THE APOLOGY AND THE LAST DAYS

The Apology and the Last Days

A Novel

BORISLAV PEKIĆ

Translated from the Serbian by Bojan Mišić

NORTHWESTERN UNIVERSITY PRESS
EVANSTON, ILLINOIS

Northwestern University Press
www.nupress.northwestern.edu

Passages in German are reproduced as they appeared in the original Serbian edition.

Printed in the United States of America

10 9 8 7 6 5 4 3 2 1

Library of Congress Cataloging-in-Publication Data

Pekić, Borislav, 1930–1992.
[Odbrana i poslednji dani. English]
The apology and the last days : a novel / Borislav Pekić ; translated from the Serbian
by Bojan Mišić.
p. cm. — (Writings from an unbound Europe)
"First published in Serbian under the title Odbrana i poslednji dani, © 1977."
ISBN 978-0-8101-2823-1 (pbk. : alk. paper)
I. Mišić, Bojan. II. Title. III. Series: Writings from an unbound Europe.
PG1419.26.E50313 2012
891.8235—dc23

2012005925

♾ The paper used in this publication meets the minimum requirements of the American
National Standard for Information Sciences—Permanence of Paper for Printed Library
Materials, ANSI Z39.48-1992.

For Dragoslav Mihailović

And now it is time for us to go, I to death, and you to life. But which of us shall meet greater salvation is unknown to all but God.

Plato, The Apology

■ □ ■ □ ■

THE APOLOGY AND THE LAST DAYS

EXPLICATION AND A SHORT BIOGRAPHY OF ANDRIJA A. GAVRILOVIĆ, BORN IN NOVI SLANKAMEN, A SWORN LIFEGUARD OF THE DROWNING, NOW AN ÉMIGRÉ IN WEST GERMANY, SUBMITTED ALONG WITH A PETITION FOR BURIAL RIGHTS OF HIS REMAINS IN THE TERRITORY OF THE FEDERAL PEOPLE'S REPUBLIC OF YUGOSLAVIA, 1959, MUNICH, WEST GERMANY.

This manuscript is printed without any changes. Only orthographic mistakes that make ideas unclear have been corrected and edited. Sentences found in the parentheses had been crossed out by Andrija Gavrilović himself, in the belief that this act alone would nullify them. However, as they are an inseparable part of this explication, as well as a depiction of the author's mental state, the editor took the liberty, in the interest of truth, not to accede to Gavrilović's wish. Whether this was the right thing to do or not, the reader shall decide for himself. Passages crossed out with a thick layer of ink have been reconstructed with the help of a renowned forensic method. Gavrilović's German citations of Plato's *Apology* have been substituted with the translation published in Belgrade in 1970 under the title *Plato-Dialogs*, edited and translated by Miloš N. Djurić, Ph.D., and Albin Vilhar, Ph.D. The epigraph for this manuscript is the editor's. Lastly, we add to this autobiography the somewhat sentimental note that Andrija A. Gavrilović died in 1960 and, being without any family or heir to execute his last wish, in compliance with the law of the Federal Republic of Germany, was buried in the prison cemetery in Munich.

■ □ ■ □ ■

CHAPTER ONE

WHAT IMPRESSION, GENTLEMEN COMRADES, MY ACCUSERS MADE ON you, I do not know. From their oration, I—well, I hardly even recognize myself; that is how persuasive their words sounded. Even so, I would say, they have spoken not one word of truth. But what most astonished me in the many lies they told was when they warned you to be careful not to be deceived by me, because I am such a skilled speaker. Thus, as far as truth goes, they said either very little or nothing at all. While from me, you shall hear the complete truth. But I beg and implore you, gentlemen: if in my defense you sometimes hear the same words that I was in the habit of using in the public bathing place, as well as in other places, please do not be surprised. The fact is, this is my first time in a court of justice, although I am sixty years of age.

Until this morning, I had not once thought to speak nor to give any statements to anyone, although, on more than one occasion, I was approached either by Mr. Lieutenant Kulman, the federal investigator, or by Dr. Eugene Hamm, the lawyer whom the state appointed to me because I did not have enough money to pay for my defense, without which you cannot appear in a German court. Also, Comrade Ozren, from your, that is our, Federal People's Republic of Yugoslavia consulate in Munich, Germany—West, came by from time to time, offered tobacco and whatnot, and urged me to write an explication, *Erklärung,* as they say here, in which I would declare how I killed my benefactor, the Privy Councillor Mr. Erich Gruber, a wealthy manufacturer, because I had found out somewhere about his involvement in a massacre during the last war in your, that is our, country (while it was still called the Mother Serbia).

"Since we laid our arms to rest, we can't do anything to them anymore," said Comrade Ozren. "Germany is still chock-full of them. They watch each other's back, the bastards, protecting one another. But you, my old man, if you weren't such a yellowbelly, you could inflame the public."

"Who am I to inflame the public?"

"You, old man, are the victim of fascist terror."

"No, I'm not," I resisted. "I'm nobody's victim."

"What are you talking about, old man? Sure you are; except you don't know it yet."

"Fine," I conceded in the end. "Even if I am, I'm only my own victim, the victim of my oafish head."

"And you could be, if you were just a tad smarter, a fascist victim, too."

"Perhaps I could," said I. "But what for?"

"It would blow up."

"What do I care if it blows up?"

"It would be taken into consideration during the sentencing," he continued probing just as he had been accustomed to do. "They might knock off a few years."

"I could care less about a few years, Comrade Ozren. If I had cared, I wouldn't have killed."

He stared me up and down the same way the prison doctor did—as if I were mad.

"Looks like, then, you want them to finish you off."

"At least I'd be at peace," I said. "And it's just possible I would be better off. Death is one of these two: it's either such that one who dies becomes nothing and has no consciousness of anything at all, or it is like a change or a migration for the soul from here to another place."

"What are you babbling about, old man?"

"In the first case, my Comrade Ozren, death would be a gift from God because it would last no longer than a summer's night. A night without dreams. But if death is some migration from here to someplace else, and if it's true, as rumor has it, that all dead live there, what would be a greater joy than to meet your own kin again, Comrade Ozren?"

"That depends on your kin. I split up with mine in 1941. We would slaughter each other even in heaven."

"Well, now you see how things are."

"I do."

"What do you see?"

"That you're mad!" he said and spat. "You lout of a Serb!"

But he didn't give up. They never do. Since he couldn't get through one door, he, like a model comrade, tried another one. So we grappled like this until noontime of a summer's day, as the people say, although outside, as well as inside of my cell, February was in full swing. Winter cold had frozen the radiators. "We'll fix it," they said, *"am folgeden Tage."* In the meantime, I'd gathered from Ozren all kinds of newspapers, German *Zeitung*s and Serbian *Politika*s, stuffed them under my shirt and in my pants, and that way I was enduring the cold somehow, whereas he, dressed in a fur-lined coat, paced from one corner of the cell to another with steam puffing out of his mouth.

Though I was nowhere near caving under the pressure, I was wondering what it would be like if I actually had been a victim of fascist terror. I inquired how one became a victim. Some might think I was a little late, considering it's been fifteen years since the war ended. On the other hand, who wouldn't like being a weight on someone else's conscience?

"That could be arranged," promised Comrade Ozren.

"By whom?"

"Comrades," he whispered.

"And what would I have to contribute?" (I knew that with Comrade Ozren favors never came free of charge.)

"Erklärung. You must write it. Say this is how it is: I killed the bastard to take revenge. Nothing else."

"To revenge whom?"

"That also could be arranged."

I didn't accept it. I thought, if I write such an explication, everything will crumble to pieces. Right now all the pieces are in place and it couldn't be any better. If, however, I carry through with Comrade Ozren's scheme, it would be as if I hadn't done anything of my own volition, as if everything had again occurred the way others had concocted it. I'm already in my sixties, and I'm tired of living my life according to someone else's script, tired of being like stagnant water, a marsh that stirs only if someone throws a rock in it. I want for once to write my own script.

The Krauts didn't command me to write anything, except Dr. Hamm in a roundabout way and Oberleutnant Kulman, the investigator, in a more open way. I decided to sit down and write, no matter what would come of it.

These three gentlemen seemed to race each other. (Even our Savior had only one devil to contend with, where I have three of them breathing down my neck.) They knew not only what was good for me to say—if not to completely avoid my misery then to cut it in half at least—but also how to say it convincingly.

As if I cared for any of that.

Later on, around the time of the feast of Theophany, after they had given me fifteen years, along comes Lieutenant Kulman, a very odd man, who's never pleased whether you deny or confirm the charges, and starts persuading me to ease my guilty soul.

"All right," I said. "Let's ease it."

"So, *endlich*," he says with delight and starts pulling some papers out of his bag.

"I just don't know whose soul—yours or mine?"

"Yours, *natürlich*."

"Nothing's wrong with mine, Herr Oberleutnant; mine is just fine. *Sehr gut*."

"How could it be fine, *um Gottes willen*, when you've murdered a man?"

"Exactly for that reason. Because I killed him."

He took one step back and jumped as if stung by a nettle. With more sadness than severity, he said: "You're a great evildoer, old man. You are a born *Totschläger*! In my whole career, I've never seen anyone like you."

The next day, however, he's back again. Supposedly he wants to know if I have any complaints. *Danke sehr;* I don't. Am I receiving everything as prescribed by the law? *Danke sehr;* I sure am. Am I being treated lawfully? Yes. Did I change my mind regarding the explication? No, I didn't.

He attacks, and I resist. I don't want to hear anything else. What I had to say, I've already said and it's been documented. I've signed so many protocols, addenda, and inserts that I can't count them all.

Every piece of evidence checks out, and even during the investigation everyone was satisfied that the case was so neat, *alles ist so sichpassen,* that it wouldn't have to go to the higher court and cost the government more money. I was charged without any extenuating circumstances. Far from it. What rendered it more damaging was the fact that I raised my hand against the only man who was willing to help me in a foreign land, and especially the fact that I ended his life "in a particularly violent way." "While you good people," I say, "are still not sure whether you punished a guilty or an innocent man! So what sort of people are you, for God's sake?"

"The judicial sort," said Herr Oberleutnant. "*Das ist ein Rechtstaat.*" It's as if he had said that their Germany, the West one, is a real country. "Unlike in your Serbia, where our soldiers and even the prisoners protected under the Hague Conventions were beaten without any consideration for the niceties of law."

"I know nothing about that, Sir. I had fled and I've never been in a place where soldiers protected under the Hague Conventions were beaten and battered. But, perhaps, there was a reason for it."

"You're a Red, old man!" he yelled. "You're a Communist!"

"If I were a Red, would I be wandering around Germany?"

"Yes, you are, old man. Admit it! Your friends from the consulate, they coerced you into killing!"

"What kind of friends are they? And nobody coerced me into anything," I rebutted. "Nobody!"

"So why did you kill?"

"Just because. Does anyone ask why it rains or why the grass grows?"

"Even the grass doesn't grow from unsown ground, if we are going to philosophize! You, old man, the way you are, you could never orchestrate such a thing. Your communists taught you, and now they're washing their hands and letting you suffer for them."

"That's not the way it was, Herr Oberleutnant!"

"Yes, it was!"

"No, it wasn't, Sir, on my life!"

Kulman lowered his voice so that I could hardly hear it. As if he was not talking to me but struggling with his thoughts.

"But if that had been the way it happened, you see, you wouldn't have gotten even five years. You might have walked with a suspended sentence."

"How?"

"That could have been arranged."

"I know," I said. "The comrades could have arranged it."

"What damned comrades, you idiot!" he exploded. "The gentlemen can arrange it! Write the *Erklärung* and say you were influenced. Everything else is our responsibility."

"And who influenced me?"

"You know who, don't play dumb!"

"I don't know unless you tell me."

"I have nothing to tell you," he said evasively, the son of a bitch. "You want me to tell you so that later you can say that we led you to lie."

A little later, though, he said that the Yugoslav consulate has many people inside. I must know someone, since I've—and they know everything—knocked at their door numerous times.

"I know only Comrade Ozren; I talked to him regarding repatriation."

"There!" he beamed. "That Ozren was the one who convinced you. He promised you a safe journey back home only if you kill Mr. Privy Councillor."

Strangely enough, even Comrade Ozren had suggested that I say I was a Red. Granted, he didn't want me to be a member. On the contrary, he said being a Serb—a Yugoslav was bad enough—and being part of the organization would make it even worse. In the state of the world, this would be the last thing I needed.

"But," he said, "it would be nice if you were a working man, a downtrodden worker. The best would be a downtrodden worker who gained consciousness."

"And what was I until now?"

"A sheep," he said. "A millstone around the neck of history."

"All right," I answered. "I'd rather be a millstone around history's neck than the other way around."

This is how, honestly, without any lies, everything revolved around Redness. First he attempted to persuade me that my benefactor, Mr. Councillor, was a war criminal listed in the Nuremberg files and that your, that is our, people would have unequivocally liquidated him if the son of a bitch had not run away. I said that I was clueless about all of it and that Mr. Gruber had always been very good to me, was never a war criminal to me, and, as far as I know, never a war criminal to anyone else.

"If we say he was, then he was."

"Even if he was, who cares? I surely didn't hold his hand."

"Of course he was. From the files it jumps right out that he was."

"What files?"

"The government files. You see, old man, the government is like one big corporation. To survive, it has to keep a good ledger of its products. There's an item for every citizen."

"Mr. Councillor Gruber was not a citizen."

"No, but we're greatly indebted to him, so we put him with the honorary ones. There's something on you, too, Gavrilović, don't you worry about that."

"That's good," I said. "Now you can cross me out."

"We never cross anybody out, so don't talk nonsense, old man. If it turns out that Gruber liquidated anyone from your family, the court would consider this during the deposition. You would scrape through by the skin of your teeth and in ten years start afresh."

"When you're in your sixties, you don't start afresh, Comrade Ozren."

"You'd walk while you're still in your seventies. At least you would be buried in your home ground."

"That's something," I agreed. "But he didn't kill anyone from my family."

"That could be arranged."

"How?"

"Easily. Why do you think the *Apparat* exists?"

"What can the *Apparat* do when I didn't have anyone anyway?"

"Don't tell me that a thunderbolt forged you out of stone."

"I did have a mother, but the woman died in 1943 when our guys took Stalingrad."

"There you go. That bastard killed your mother."

"The old lady died from intestinal infection."

"Even that could be arranged."

"I can't," I said. "I can't accuse an innocent man. He was like a father to me. He gave me a job in the worst of times. He accepted me almost as one of his own. It's not humane to accuse a dead man."

"And breaking his skull—that you can do, and that is humane? So why the fuck did you kill him then, if he was such a saint?"

Everyone asked the same question. Everyone got stuck on the same thing: Was he good to me? Yes. So why did you kill him then? I'm telling you people, there was some special bond between us. Were there harsh words between you? No, there was something worse. Like what? That, I can't tell you. Why not? I've sworn not to say anything. And you judges can send me to prison, or kill me, do whatever you want to me, just don't ask me anymore. The anguish I felt was my own and had nothing to do with him. He was always good to me.

"An employer can never be good," said Ozren.

"This one was."

"He was a capitalist bloodsucker."

"No, he wasn't, Comrade Ozren."

"That vampire cut your paycheck short; he wouldn't let you join the union, and he treated you like a dog until you sweated blood! That's why you killed him! You killed him as an enemy of the working class."

"No, I didn't!" I objected. "It's useless to bring up the working class!"

But if I had latched onto the working class, I might have swum out of the whole thing in one piece. You may even think that the verdict came out the way it did because I did not use the words I could have used had I decided to exploit every means to avoid punishment. Although I was guilty because of poverty, it's better if I talk about things more soothing to hear; to wail and weep, and to say and do anything else, is, I think, unworthy of me.

And so I did not want to write an explication, not when the sentence was pronounced, nor after the appeal confirmed the sentence, nor even after they locked me up in prison.

Inzwischen, the insolent Mr. Kulman still did not stop coming to my cell, trying to convince me. Always the same thing: just write it and ease your soul! As if he was a priest and not a cop. Here, in Germany, you have cops who are like our village priests. Everything, up to the final breath, they want to know. They want to dot every *i*.

"Why are you always coming to see me, Herr Oberleutnant? What else do you want?"

"The truth."

II
▾

"What truth? What is truth? Just a thread. A fine thread. So fine, you couldn't even thread the whole thing through the eye of the needle."

"What are you, Gavrilović: a philosopher or a fool?"

"Both. But I would never have become a philosopher if I hadn't been a fool first."

"Aren't you sorry for your life?"

"I haven't lived it, so I can't say."

But after all, I didn't write the explication. Nor even did I send an appeal. What for? I was all right with how everything turned out. I was finally given a word, and I wanted to keep it, like a real man.

But here, my lawyer, Dr. Hamm—the Devil take him—jumped in. Just as if they were all in cahoots. Whenever one of them left me alone, another would seize me in his hands. The German gentlemen, Mr. Kulman and Dr. Hamm, worked in concert with Comrade Ozren from the consulate. They didn't mind that he was a Communist, and he, at least for this occasion, was not bothered by capitalism. They sifted me from hand to hand, as if I were a crumb of costly ore for which it would be a shame to blow away before it was speckled over some high governmental aim.

Even though I didn't ask him to, and even specifically requested him not to, Dr. Hamm, on his own initiative, pulled together the appeal for my case: So, the prisoner is an older man, and life has given him the hardest and most inevitable sentence. Even though this man has spent a lot of time outside his country, he, on the other hand, has not lived long in German civilization. He is confused, a poor soul, *sehr geehrte Herr Richtern,* Your Honor. As if I was feebleminded or something, that's how it was written. And furthermore, and I am quoting, that I was "unprepared to be exposed to the pressures of a highly industrialized society." I have the copy of it with me. It sounded, according to them, as if I had just yesterday climbed down from a tree, or that I was born in the woods and not in a town that even had a movie projector, though for sure only in the wintertime. "It's the Balkans, *sehr geehrte Herren,* a wilderness. Just remember Sarajevo and the year of 1914," he said. "Remember the bestial way in which they whacked His Highness, the honorable Archduke Ferdinand and his Duchess Sophie. And, since we are on the subject of national customs, they even threw their own kings out the windows!

They did not respect the Hague Conventions. During the war they slaughtered each other like wolves. And now, *sehr geehrte Herr Richtern,* they use and abuse our German hospitality to settle their old accounts. It is as if we do not have any laws, or as if the laws do not even faze them at all. Frankly speaking," said Dr. Hamm, "they have no regard for the constitution. And this is the primary factual verity that the lower court did not fully take into consideration during the ruling. For they"—meaning we, to be precise—"abide by different laws." There was, allegedly, some man, a chief by the name of Dukadjini. I, however, have never heard of such a man, and, what's more, I think Hamm made it all up in double time just for the plea bargain, figuring that Serbia is God knows where and that no one would verify his story. So that same Dukadjini created a law called Lex, according to which their, meaning our, primary pride and boast was to revenge our wounded honor with blood. And if we didn't do that, if we chickened out, the whole society would hold us in ignominy forever.

"This is why, Your Honor, my defendant, Andreas Gavrilović," meaning myself, "had to kill the deceased Herr Geheimer Gruber if he did not want to be, in his primitive world, considered less of a person and seen as an emasculated man, and so you could and so you must consider this reason in light of the most recent research on primitive clan mentality; he did not kill Herr Gruber, Herr Gruber was killed by the barbaric state of soul and customs in which his compatriots live." The dramatist spelled all this out in his plea bargain. This is how he characterized me: as bad as some kind of dark barbarian straight out of Albania. Even though what he said clearly lacked any truth, he thought he uttered it for my own good.

And when I asked him why he filed an appeal when I, its suffering subject, was satisfied, he said that this is how it must be according to the *Gesetz* in Germany, the Western one. And there, *Gesetz* means Law. *Gesetz* is the Law, and *Gesetzbuch* is the Code from which they interpret it, from which they proclaimed my fifteen years, too, and from which they, just as Mr. Kulman did, reminded me that this is a juridical country. *Das ist ein Rechtstaat.*

I did not protest. If this is their *Gesetz,* why jump up and down protesting? Regarding the murder, the most important thing to me was that I was in control, and they could write all kinds of documents and addenda.

And yet, here I am, alone in my cell, writing the explication on my own volition. They have already washed their hands of me. They realized they were wasting their time with a dope.

Even Comrade Ozren from the Yugoslav consulate in Munich spat and said, "I hope you choke in prison, you fucking lout!"

Before he left, he snatched back a pack of cigarettes he'd brought for me. I guess he didn't want to waste his cigarettes on such a muddleheaded guy. But I saw he felt sorry about it. I guess because we are still countrymen. He left that pack of cigarettes with the warden to give them back.

It was also hard for Dr. Hamm. He screamed and yelled at me so much, he came close to thumping me. He told me all kinds of things right to my face. He said I was a scoundrel and an ass. *Dummkopf. Du bist ein Balkanischer Dummkopf!* When I asked him why he cared and worried about it, since I was the one committed for fifteen years and it is my life, he said that he didn't want his office to be a gateway to prison. This could ruin his name and reputation in the country.

"We could've gotten away with a maximum of five years," he said.

"How?"

"If you had just listened to me and pretended you were dumbheaded. That wouldn't even be far from the truth because you are a lunatic. To raise your hand against your patron, to slaughter a chicken that produces eggs, that only a *serbische Dummkopf* could do."

He, unfortunately, was a nonsmoker, so he did not leave any cigarettes. He went away to worry about someone else. He left, saying, "I might work with tougher criminals somewhere, but certainly not with dumber."

Only Mr. Oberleutnant Kulman said nothing. He stared me up and down with those watery eyes of his and shook his head as if he did not understand anything.

And he didn't. Nobody here ever understands anything.

And I am writing this against my initial decision, not because I was told this morning, bright and early, that the lawyer's appeal, the one with Franz Ferdinand, Dukadjini, and other such nonsense, was rejected, and that for me, as they said, there was no other lawful way out. That is not the reason. The reason is that during the investigation I visited the prison library. The room was gargantuan. Everywhere around me were books on the shelves. So many books in one place,

I've never seen before. I was looking around, leafing through some of them, searching for the ones with pictures. There were some like that, but they were even harder to understand. The librarian tried to explain to me that those were art pictures. What kind of pictures are they when you can't see anything in them. There were even some editions in Fraktur which I couldn't read. I don't know Fraktur. I had a hard enough time battling with contemporary German script; I had to learn it for the sake of bookkeeping. All of a sudden I saw a book that, according to its title, had something to do with a court case: *The Apology and the Last Days of Socrates* by some Plato guy. I froze. It's impossible! Plato was my priest in Novi Slankamen. That he'd conducted a good liturgy and had made a name amongst the women, so much I knew. But that he had written books, I sure didn't know that. And, of course, he hadn't. The language in the book seemed folksy without any claptrap. Let's see what it is all about, I thought, and if there is any use for it; in particular, because the book was about defense in the court of law. Even though I didn't defend myself, I thought it would be useful to know how the clever people do it. I checked out the book, took it to my cell, and read it through several times. I realized quickly that Socrates was my brother in sorrow, accused in the name of God. He was charged for not believing in the same gods that the state did, but believing in other, demonic beings. And as for me, similarly, during the war I'd signed a pact with the Devil. Of course the difference is that Socrates defended himself vigorously, and I did not. But that didn't get him very far. Both of us were sentenced; in his case, to death. He had to drink a poison made from hemlock.

As I was reading his recitation, it came to my mind that I should write down the truth about my own case, so that when I die, nobody could create any lies about me. This was my reason to write, not some kind of search for a legal way out, because, as they had said, there were none anymore. I have to go to prison, but the day and the hour have not yet been decided, not until they figure it out. In that respect, I have nothing to worry about. Everyone says that here the execution comes very fast, so I do not worry. Some time has passed since I worried last. All I had been doing was worrying.

Even now I wouldn't take up writing except that the idea of coming back to my homeland, even in a casket, has gotten stuck in my head, and Socrates's defense taught me how to achieve this. I had inquired about the whole procedure even before, through Comrade Ozren. I had found that with my request I would need to enclose a short biography: what kind of work you have done and where, who of your family is abroad, and what they've done while living there. (I've written such short biographies for Comrade Ozren numerous times; I was tired of writing anymore. He, on the other hand, never had enough of them. He combed through everything, cross-checked everything, and compared every detail. "Here you wrote this," he said, "and there you wrote that! In the last biography you said you spent two years in Hanover, and here you said twenty-three months! Explain, you schemer of an emigrant, where did you spend that month and how?" I became so lost that I knew neither where and when I was born nor what my name was.)

This writing of mine is not going to be short, since my agony was not short either, and I am going to say not only just what happened where, but also why it happened and what I, Andrija Gavrilović, think about it.

Because what impression my accusers made on you, I don't know, just as that Socrates didn't know. From their oration I—well, I hardly even recognize myself; that is how persuasive their words sounded. Yet, I would say, they have spoken not one word of truth. But what most astonished me in the many lies they told was when they warned you to be careful not to be deceived by me, because I am such a skilled speaker. Thus, as far as truth goes, they either said very little or nothing at all. But from me, you shall hear the complete truth.

As soon as everyone heard that I had changed my mind, Mr. Lieutenant Kulman ran to my cell, bringing me lined paper, pen and ink, and even a few extra pens, as well as a red leather piece, soft as your skin, to put under the paper. And the whole time he was prancing around, asking me if my bed was comfortable to lie on and if I could use a pillow or two? Or if I would like some coffee? Sleep, he said, destroys awareness, so he would order a pot of fresh coffee to be available for me at any time. And even though alcohol was not allowed, he would inquire if something could be done regarding that as well. He would not leave me alone. And I, once more, just couldn't get to work. He only left when I told him that I'd backslide if he didn't leave me alone. As he was leaving, he stopped at the door to remind me not to hurry at all, but say everything from the beginning to the end, as if I were just now arrested in Ammersee, and also, to be sure by any means not to forget to mention—and I would know in what sense—Ozren from the consulate.

Dr. Hamm, of course, came by as well. He recommended I take this opportunity and steer our case—he meant my case, but for some reason he thought of it as his as well—in the right direction.

"Listen to me, Andreas," he said. "It would be best to say that on that particular day you were indisposed."

"And what is that?" I asked.

"*Überspannt.* Out of your wits, crazy. You could say that you have recurrent headaches."

"Well, I do have recurrent headaches."

"There you go. The case is clear. Herr Geheimer Kommerzienrat scolded you for not cleaning the pool; you blamed it on the unbearable pain in your head, he denied your explanation, there were words, you somehow provoked him, and so he started beating you with a stick."

"And then?"

"And then because of the insults and all those Dukadjini laws, you, *überspannt Mensch,* snatched the stick and, in the struggle that ensued, cracked his head. But you remember neither the details nor your actions, you blanked out, and so you don't remember *nichts.* You only came to in the police station."

Then again, he went on about the Balkans and the primitive mentality, about German civilization and other such nonsense, and then he left, saying that from now on he would start visiting me more often.

After them came Comrade Ozren from your, I mean our, consulate. (This guy, more than anyone else, got on my nerves. He was a real weight on my shoulders.) He brought me cigarettes, supposedly to have them handy while I reflected. As soon as he opened the door, he said:

"Don't worry about anything, old man. I know what to do!"

"What?"

"I know how it happened and how you killed him."

"Even I know that."

"You don't know anything, you dumb ox!" I don't want to bore you with the whole story. Good Comrade Ozren concocted it in order to rescue me, while at the same time contributing to the country.

And then again, why shouldn't I tell you the whole story anyway?

I've never been a pundit. I'm not Socrates either. I have a few years of schooling and a head on my shoulders. It's enough for me to see who's who and what's what. I see, for example, that Comrade Ozren is good for nothing. Neither for consular work nor for showing himself in public. Maybe he could be useful around the house, I don't know, but he shouldn't be allowed to cross the border. Not even to Trieste. He speaks German, and that's all right, although he never gets the genders right. Everyone's constantly asking him to repeat what he says. So he always has a translator with him. According to him this is the rule in diplomatic circles, seemingly to gain time. I'll give him that one, but I think it is because he does not know German very well.

Sooner or later, he's going to bury the country in some deep shit. That much is clear. Even though I don't count as a citizen of Yugoslavia anymore, it's still my homeland and I care about it. It's my duty to speak truthfully, and the truth is that Ozren is not made for diplomacy. Maybe to guard the consulate's gate.

But I am truly grateful for the cigarettes, even though he squashed half of them in anger.

And so he said that I'm a dumb ox who knows nothing.

"All right," I said.

It's useless to bicker with a scoundrel. Better to let them have their way. The sooner he says what is on his mind, the sooner he'll leave. Otherwise he would've shouted all day—he could wail like a factory siren—and he would've taken my tobacco as well. And I craved tobacco more than bread. I couldn't even think straight without it.

"Was there a bar at the place that dog admitted you?"

"There was, and a pretty big one," I said. "Rows and rows of bottles."

"Good," he said happily. "This means he was already sozzled."

"But Comrade Ozren, that guy didn't drink. He was a family man with a good reputation."

"Those are the worst ones. I know the type well. I have those in the consulate, too, but not for much longer. They drink secretly, especially if something is eating them up."

"What was eating the councillor?"

"What do you mean what? His war crimes, of course. That's why he drank so much. When you arrived, he was drunk as a pig."

"He wasn't," I said. But, I thought, let's see what's going to come out of this.

"Yes, he was. Don't play dumb, you fucker."

"I'm not playing dumb. I just want it to be known what kind of a man he was and that the murder didn't have anything to do with him."

"What kind of a man he was? Just like this—nothing. An egotist. Drank by himself, didn't offer you any. Didn't even invite you to sit down."

"He was in a hurry, and he wasn't even sitting down."

"While standing, the bastard started to insult you and to cuss your whore of a Bolshevik mother."

"Why would he call *my* mother that? She was a decent and a smart woman; she didn't abuse anyone."

"Because of where you're from, because you reminded him of the ones he'd slaughtered and put in mass graves."

"I don't know that Mr. Gruber slaughtered anyone."

"He hated you, it's obvious."

"Then why did he keep me around?"

"That's exactly why."

"That's pretty darn complicated."

"Of course it is. They told us in school that every criminal gets all mixed up and that every one of them always comes back to the crime scene."

"But I am the victim, what would I do at the crime scene?"

"This is true for a victim as well."

"Now I understand."

"And it was about time. Now, things were moving pretty fast. He yelled how you should've been slaughtered along with the rest of the Communist pigs, how they should've shot every one of you. Then he began to boast, and with a smile on his face—that damned blood-hound—of how many he'd killed with his own hand. Especially when he started talking about women and children. Do you, Andrija, have any kids?"

"Yes, I do," I said. "I have one, but it's as if I don't have one."

"*Gut,*" he said. "To spice it up a little, the best thing would be to say that somewhere he ordered—and we'll decide where later—to burn someone's house down. Picture this: the house is burning, and through the door comes a woman carrying a child pressed against her bosom, and he, the monster, orders the child to be thrown into the flames right in front of the mother. Later, of course, he liquidated the mother as well, with a bullet from a Parabellum right in the back of the head. And that's when all hell broke loose. That's when you, my man, had had enough. You grabbed a stick and beat him to death. Then you dragged his limp body and threw him in the pool."

That was Comrade Ozren's plan. All I had to do was to write it down neatly, and public opinion would take care of the rest. I'd be out of jail and of some use for the country.

"What do you mean, 'use,' for God's sake?" I asked. I can never make heads or tails of high-level politics.

"It's of the greatest importance!" said Comrade Ozren, while twining around me like a grapevine. All the time, he whispered, fearing that some *Volksdeutscher* who spoke our language might be amongst the guards and would mess up his plan. The fear and everything else he spat out on that occasion convinced me completely that he does not belong in the consulate of the Federal People's Republic of Yugoslavia, but in a mental institution, and that if he continues in this way, he's going to create a huge international hubbub.

"There are," he said, "some heavy negotiations about awarding war reparations to the victims of fascist terror. Those bastards, the Krauts, are bargaining hard. They wiggle around the numbers we had submitted: one million eight hundred thousand dead souls, and not even considering the lame and crippled ones. They're asking for arbitration. They argue that we fought amongst ourselves, and even those who died from old age or from some illness are now counted and placed on their bill. They say we also included the traitors, the ones we liquidated in Slovenia near Bleiburg and in Bosnia in 1945—and some of them we really did—and also all the people killed by every possible German collaborator, all kinds of lowlife that, as you know, existed back then, and that they couldn't have, even if they'd wanted to, killed so many people in only four years; neither in four nor in forty. And we, Comrade Andrija, need money. The country is in ruins, and our five-year plan is huge. And then there is electrification and industrialization to consider—we don't want to be an imperial colony again, so that everyone can suck lead and wood out of us—and money is nowhere to be found. This year's harvest was a whorish disappointment, the Russians swindled us, and the Americans give to us in bits and pieces. It's enough to drive you insane. So with all that, build your future if you can. Now, do you see what this is all about, Comrade Andrija?"

"I see the hardship," I said, "but I don't see where I fit into these global politics."

"As a member of the global proletariat. The country of workers and peasants is in question, and you, Comrade Andrija, you are a worker."

"I was a sworn lifeguard of the drowning," I said. "I don't know where I belong."

"You belong to the proletariat, of course. But don't get too cocky."

"I'm not being cocky. I just don't know how I can help."

"Great; the more that's written about war crimes, the better for us. We need to stir up the populace and soften the Germans. So write whatever you're told, and don't you worry about the rest. Later on, you can even create that petition for burial rights. I'll personally take care of your corpse."

"And what happens if I don't write what you've told me?"

"Then we won't even take your corpse."

This is what I wanted you to know about Comrade Ozren, so you can take actions accordingly.

I finally told everyone that I would do as they had asked me, but the whole time I was carrying my own tune.

At last they let me alone. Except for the guard who brought meals, no one else came. Only once in a while someone would ask me if I needed anything. I'm sure it was Mr. Oberleutnant Kulman who ordered them to do it.

It was arranged for them to personally come for the explication. Kulman told me not to send it through the guard by any means, only to place it into his own hands. Dr. Hamm, as my lawyer, would come as well, since I promised him a copy, and, of course, another one to Comrade Ozren from the Yugoslav consulate in Munich. He was supposed to be the only one who would get it, or at least this was the arrangement.

And as for me, God willing, I won't give it to anyone, neither to Kulman, nor to Hamm, nor to Ozren. I'll fold and seal it in an official blue envelope, with a note that it is not to be opened by anyone until my death, and only when I die, let it be airmailed to the marshal himself in Belgrade.

And so, everything will end as it was destined to be, which is best for everybody. This time it will be only according to my wishes, unlike the way it always has been. Someone else was always pulling me their way, and I just stood around and watched. It seems you have a life, but you really don't. You're alive, seemingly, and therefore you live, but you can throw it all to hell if the life isn't really yours, if you are not the steersman. Now I'm at the helm. I'm holding on tight with both hands, and I'll never let go whatever might happen.

It's also right to say, although I'm not guilty, that I've deserved all of this. I deserved this to happen to me, and so it did happen. My father was a simple and uneducated man. He was a fisherman, a real waterman, and people say water makes one clairvoyant—me, it did not make such; otherwise, I wouldn't be in jail. Stories tell of seers always being near water, and, as it is known, the greater the body of water is, the clearer you can see. And my father was a quiet and a sad man. You would never see him angry or happy. He drifted, if I may say, like the tranquil river in which he fished. He used to say that a happy man is one who gets what he deserves (good or bad, it doesn't matter), and that the happy life is the deserved one. All things considered, mine will be one like that.

This thing did not happen to me by sheer coincidence. It's obvious that the best thing for me would be to die right now and free myself from misery. For this reason no inner voice ever stopped me, and I am personally not angry at those who condemned me. Even without their judgment I would have only another year to live, and so in a short time their wishes would be fulfilled. There are also other circumstances that help me not to be angry at the judgment that has befallen me.

Therefore, you should know that I am not pleading for *my* own sake, as one might expect, but for yours, so that *you* will not condemn me and, in that way, will not sin against the only gift given to us by God.

■ □ ■ □ ■

CHAPTER TWO

MY NAME IS ANDRIJA GAVRILOVIĆ, BORN OF A FATHER NAMED ANDRIJA, now deceased and better known as "the aqueous one" because in the same region there was already a person with the same name but known as "the earthen one," and of a mother named Bojana, née Krstushky, now deceased, from Novi Slankamen on the Danube, County of Mitrovica, District of Srem, Republic of Serbia, Federal People's Republic of Yugoslavia. Here in Germany I was rechristened to Andreas, and under such a Germanic name I was entered into their books, in the court records, and in the documentation for the residence and social welfare. I am writing this explication from the prison in Munich, West Germany, the country where I have been living since the fall of 1944, which means fourteen years, five months, and a few days, including this one as well.

Before this, I lived in Lübeck and even before that in Hanover and Hamburg. I was even in Travemünde for a short time, *ja.* As is well known, Travemünde is Germany's most luxurious summer resort on the Baltic Sea—I personally was frozen to the bones there. And on the other sea, the North Sea, lies Hamburg, although it is not very clear on the map and even less clear in person just how much of the sea touches the city. It's as if they stretched out some lake and slapped together the port from its bottom. Frankfurt and Mainz, where I resided briefly, are near the water as well. All this, where I lived and where I stayed, I reported on numerous occasions to Comrade Ozren from the consulate in Munich without omitting anything, although

I've repeated it so many times I probably added something. It could be verified that I did not conceal anything that happened to me since my misfortunes began, and since my oafish head led me away from Serbia and its waters.

I was born on the water, and grew up on the water. My father Andrija was, as I said before, a fisherman, but, judging by our sad life, the fish did not in particular go his way. My mother kept us afloat by working as a seamstress. Apparently, the needle did not go her way either—nobody needed sewing in those days—so we, the children, were forced to labor, too. We helped out my father and other fishermen with their nets. We took care of them, mended cast and drift nets, netted coops out of wicker, and untangled baits. Other fishermen had some luck, but my father had none whatsoever. Maybe the seasons were such that the fish did not bite no matter how hard my father tried. Later on, luck was no friend of mine either, so I realized how hard it must have been for my father, although I was not so considerate when I was young. I had thought my father was not skillful enough and that I would do better, no matter what job I would take up.

I never finished any school. Everything I know of science, I learned by myself. I did, however, start elementary school, but just then World War I started and I was pulled out to toil tilling on a farm. My father was recruited immediately, of course. My mother did not have any sewing work because nobody was in the mood for fashion. I don't even know how many forints they paid me. The job was suited more for a horse than for a man. Ever since I've hated the soil; I can't even look at it.

During the Battle of Cer, my father was captured by you, I mean, by us. He was immediately transferred to the Serbian army, but he didn't get a chance to fire even one bullet. He contracted typhus during the retreat and barely survived in one piece. After the war and the declaration of our glorious kingdom, he came back home and continued to fish. But he never really recovered; he always looked withered and dispirited. In the end, a strong wind caught him in the middle of the river and he drowned. He didn't know how to swim. Back then not too many people swam, not even fishermen. The river washed him ashore three days later. We barely recognized him. My mother somehow recognized him. I don't know how she did it, she never told us. "It's him," was all she said. I'll never forget the way he looked: completely washed-out, blanched and blue as if rotten. This image, I think, had an immense influence in my choosing my profession.

Soon after, I came to the realization that if I stayed I'd waste my whole life slaving for a stranger. I left the house and my hometown, and at first I arrived in Zemun and then in Belgrade. Finally, I settled down in a town, whose name I don't wish to mention—it's all in Comrade Ozren's records. There, gentlemen comrades, I did everything. Just like any other proletarian, I worked for hourly wages. I worked unloading coal in a harbor and mixing concrete at construction sites. The main chief was Constantine Negovan, but everyone called him "the Wolf." He was a gargantuan man, both in body and in voice, partially the boss and partially a man of the people who worked along with us, whether you were a newcomer or not. I worked as a brickmaker, baking clay—a hell of a tiring job—and also as a luggage carrier at railroad stations until I was thrown out because I was working illegally. Right after the war, during the epidemic, I even worked as a gravedigger. We were buried with work at that time. Some kind of Spanish fever had hit so strong that Serbs were dying in heaps.

Then I saw a county poster calling for all young, healthy, and strong people to enlist, for a decent salary, for the noble job of a lifeguard to save people at the local beaches and public pools. All they required was that a person had served in the army, which I had, and that he be a good swimmer, which I also was. I didn't think twice. I applied and with a few others was chosen for the job.

In the beginning they started to teach us all kinds of things. Most of all they taught us artificial respiration, how to use a first aid kit, the best responses in various aquatic emergencies, and how to knock out a victim in distress with one hit if he resists too much. In short, they taught us things I hadn't even dreamed about.

(It's not just jumping in the water and pulling a man out on dry land. Also it doesn't help if you come straight at him; he'll try to grab you and then you'll both drown, especially if you're tired from swimming too fast. Of course you must swim fast; we're talking about saving a living soul, but you can't do it impetuously. You must have good swimming strength and swim fast with even strokes. If you can, the best way to approach a victim is from behind and the worst is from the side. And you want to grab him under the armpit. This is known as a "nelson." Also, mouth-to-mouth resuscitation is not so simple either. It's not just swinging his arms and that's it. First you must lay the victim on his stomach, place a rock underneath him, empty mud, if any, out of his mouth, tie his tongue to his chin, and empty water out of his lungs and stomach. Only after that can you proceed with blowing air into his lungs.)

So after they instructed me what to do, I was put to work. I worked as a sworn lifeguard until I fled to West Germany.

Also, even in Germany I worked at various strands, which is what they call bathing places, beaches, and spas. My status, however, wasn't always of an official lifeguard; I didn't always work *als ein Retter*, even though at home this was my only profession. I functioned also as a simple *Wächter*, a cabin attendant, and, even worse, as a pool cleaner. After a while it got better and finally it got really good. *Sehr gut. Sehr gut, natürlich*, considering all the circumstances. I advanced. Owing to my benefactor, the one they said I murdered, Geheimer Kommerzienrat Gruber, I was positioned to serve as a night guard at the swimming pool in Schwabing in Munich. Later Mr. Gruber took me to work for him. All I had to do was to oversee his summer villa in the mountains in nearby Ammersee.

Therefore, I was no longer a lifeguard, but a former lifeguard. I was getting up there in years, and the recession was all around. And then there was my crippled hand. It didn't bother me in the beginning. Only once in a while, I would feel a sharp pain in my elbow, and then my shoulder would get numb. Later on, it got worse and developed some arthritis, so I couldn't go into the water anymore. Although for me, that did not bother me that much as long as I was *next* to water. Since it drowned my father, water somehow had become part of me. It was probably for this reason that I chose it as my profession. If I'd only had the chance to oversee our native Serbian water instead of some foreign one, I would've been a happy man.

This, however, is no one's fault but mine. I don't mean what happened to me now. It is true that I'm in a real predicament, but I don't care a bit about it. For my present crime, I don't feel guilty at all. I know that everybody expects me to write only about that: how and why I killed Herr Geheimer Kommerzienrat Gruber. I, on the other hand, only think about my true crime, the one that forced me to flee from my country and wander around the world, and about my past accusers who led me here.

Remember that there are two different sets of plaintiffs who are against me: the ones who have charged me now and the other ones of whom I spoke of earlier. Now, if you think about it, it is more appropriate to answer the older accusations first. They are numerous and the plaintiffs have been doing their business for a long time; they addressed you at times when you were most vulnerable because a good number of you were either only children or young boys, and for that reason their accusations are good for nothing. I was already in exile in Germany. And what is even more bizarre is that I don't even know their names. And all of those who gained your confidence out of envy and out of their passion for slandering, as well as those who were themselves persuaded and therefore tried to persuade others, all of these are the least accessible ones since I can bring none of them to court to discredit them as witnesses.

You may ask, and I do not resent you for it: where did all those accusations come from? Don't tell us that you haven't done anything wrong. In that case, Andrija Gavrilović, your name would not have become so well known, not unless you differed from others and had done different things than all your countrymen!

And that's the truth; I'm not trying to refute or muddy it. All I want is to explain and put everything in the right context. Great is my crime, so great that you can neither put it in words nor imagine it even halfway. Nothing will ever be clear. Even I don't fully understand it, so how can anyone else? The only certain thing is the magnitude of my sin, and I am ashamed to even talk about it. As if being nameless or unrecognizable makes the sin less significant. This, however, is not the case. Although, I have to say that until the war I had never heard of it. It seems that it did not exist before, as if it was discovered and named only then. It is a strange kind of sin that at one moment exists and at another doesn't; sometimes it ends well and sometimes it turns into evil. Even the first time I heard its name, I didn't understand its meaning. (The Holy Scriptures do not mention it under this name; I looked it up. Only later did I realize that it was there, except that it's called the Pact with the Devil, conniving and cooperating with demons, of which the aforementioned Socrates was accused as well.) This was something foreign for us. Apparently the sin was so great that we didn't have a domestic name for it, so we had to borrow a foreign one and christen it after someone named Quisling, who it seems invented it. That Quisling was the head of the government, similar to our General Nedić. I was never the head of a government, but I was still a quisling. A lesser one, of course, and not as great as the initial creator of the name, but this, nevertheless, was enough to be labeled as one after the war. There was also another name for my unsuitability, and even that one was not Serbian. As if the Serbs before me had never done anything similar, so they did not require a name for it. So my thing was called collaboration, which means, in Serbian of course, cooperation with an aggressor. In the German language, as I see it, it means nothing wicked. For example, while I worked as a cabin keeper in Munich I had to collaborate with the pool authorities, and no one saw anything wrong with it. Not even the labor union and they were always a little tense. In Serbian, however, this word has developed into a cataclysm.

So this is how all of us who have sinned in the same fashion became quislings, collaborators and cooperators with the enemy, which in this case meant the Germans. Not with these Germans of today, of course not; now it is even commendable to work with them. I'm talking about their fathers. Domestic traitors, fascists, enemies of the people, occupiers' vassals, and according to Comrade Ozren: bastards, trash, *Auswurfs,* and shitheads. The worst shit possible.

And how I became a collaborator and an enemy vassal, I shall disclose here, even though it may seem unrelated to my current crime. You shall see, however, that it is of the greatest importance, that the one cannot be understood without the other, and truthfully this one would not have happened without the first one.

You normally want to understand everything. As a matter of fact, everybody wants to understand. This, they say, is their purpose. They are not so much after justice, and even less after punishment, as much as they are after understanding. Oberleutnant Kulman has often said to me, "I could care less, Gavrilović, about ascertaining anything from you. All I want is to comprehend you. Everything I needed for the court, I've gotten it a long time ago, but I still haven't figured you out." He also added, and I remember clearly every word, "A true verdict in a criminal case can be reached only if the real causes can be ascertained, and these are hidden behind conspicuous facts, which act as the invisible machine. For a good court of justice, facts are soulless puppets until the trial unravels all the threads that manipulate the puppets on the criminal scene, until the court understands the machine that directs the criminal play from behind the curtain. Until then, justice has to toil with a phantom because its scales weigh an unbalanced weight." This is how Oberleutnant Kulman talked, all the while trying to place those secret threads into the hands of Comrade Ozren, as if he was the machine that directed me in "the criminal play."

Comrade Ozren, on the other hand, was trying to place the same threads in the hands of Kulman's father, our invader. Dr. Hamm did not have much to do with that kind of politics. He leaned more toward the madness theory. It was madness that pulled all the strings and forced me to act accordingly.

As for me, I would like to dismantle that same machine the way a watchmaker dismantles a broken watch, so that all the little wheels and cogwheels become exposed and visible. Whatever happens, it would be according to my destiny and what the law prescribes.

So it happened that the county placed me as a watchman at the southern beach, where a few kilometers upstream was a northern one in which the sworn lifeguard was a chap called Zemba, a former heavyweight, a monster of a man. We were not the best of friends, and one might say we were like water and fire.

I was not friendless, however. Without an ally no one can survive. Even though my job was hard and full of responsibilities—the lives of others were in my hands—and it did not leave too much time for dawdling and carousing, I became close with a Hungarian, one called András, who was, like my deceased father, made for water. He knew so much about water that in this area no one could compare to him. I knew quite a lot myself, from what I'd learned from my father and on my own, but my knowledge was not even close to Andraš's. Zemba was a different sort. All he had going for him was his strength; he was strong as an ox, a real bone-buster, but besides that, a dimwit. I have no idea who made him a lifeguard. He knew nothing about water, as if he had grown up in the desert, or in his whole life had never even seen so much as an artesian well. It looked as if he did not care for water one bit. He was always on the lookout for some other job, something other than saving lives, which is a good indication of what kind of a man he was. He even insulted his victims. He used to say that there was nothing worse than drowning men because if you let them, they would try to drown you along with them.

"You rush to help one," he used to say, "to save his rotten soul, and all he cares for is to drag you under the water. He jumps on your back, pulling you under the waves, all along poking your eyes with his fingers. Nothing else matters to him as long as his head is above the water. And what's worse, back on land the scum doesn't even look at you, as if it was your fault that he almost drowned. He even curses at you for smacking him upside the head to calm him down to prevent both of you from drowning. Elbow! And then bam.

"I," he said, "don't even wait for them to grab me. I always smack 'em first. Why wait, I say? Once I pummeled one of them right there in the water. He almost bit off my ear. I beat the shit out of him. He would've been better off drowned."

That's how Zemba used to talk.

Besides Andraš, I was pretty good friends with the children from the suburbs. I kept my distance from the older crowd. We were still cordial of course. What can I say? It was just a part of the job. I had to keep my dignity. I was a civil servant in a uniform and under oath; I could not get involved with anyone. You are all under governmental support, so you know what could happen if a civil employee mixes up with the mob. For this reason I did not go any further than regular cordiality: "Good afternoon, Captain," "Good morning, Mrs. Marković," or "Good-bye Mrs. Trajković." It's a nice day for a swim, it is or it is not going to rain, and that was all. I'd give them a cabin key, collect the bill, carry out the lounge chairs and umbrellas, and sometimes, according to circumstance, I'd warn them to stay close to shore.

So, as I said, I did not have anything to do with the ladies and the gentlemen, but with the children and the young kids, it was different. They were always hanging around me, and I even got to look after them once in a while when their mothers had some business to take care of in town. I was always glad to do it—why not? I liked the kids. I taught them how to swim, to dive with their heads first, and even some basic water rescue skills.

If someone, either young or old, would inquire what the nature of my job was, I would never decline to respond and answer his question, and I would not do it only for money like Zemba.

That fiend Zemba, however, he would never sit quiet. He always drew the kids away from my beach. He did not care for them; he did it only to spite me, to pass his time. He had a motorboat and I just had a dory. I had one at my disposal as well, but it was only for urgent cases and not to motor kids around. Zemba, however, did not care for regulations and used his boat to drive the children away from me. I had no clue why he had it in for me. Andraš's theory was that I was that kind of a man, always asking to be trod on. I don't think that was the real reason. I've never forced an issue, that is true, and I've never defended myself either. But I've always been like that, a peaceful man.

In front of the boathouse, which served as my home as well, we had a post in the form of a scaffold made out of red painted steel, where a cowbell hung. I don't want to boast, but this was my invention. If something were to happen on the river, someone was drowning or any other catastrophe, whoever was around it would run and ring the cowbell, and I would find a way to be there. Zemba used that same cowbell to alarm me for no reason at all. I would be with the children in the house teaching them rescue skills when all of a sudden I would hear the bell. "Finally!" I'd say to myself. This was always a harmless exclamation. I did not wish for anyone to drown himself, of course, but I did want, if possible, to show myself in a good light. So I'd grab my first aid kit, run out, breaking my neck almost, when all I'd see was Zemba standing next to the cowbell, laughing like a fiend. I would get enraged. Who wouldn't?

"You, Zemba," I said trembling with anger, "respect neither people nor the service."

"And what do you want, considering my paycheck?" he said.

"Nothing. I want nothing from you. Just stay at your beach, and leave mine alone. Go and play with human lives elsewhere. You hear me?"

"I didn't come here because of you. I just want to take the kids for a spin in my boat."

And what kid could resist that? I tried my best to keep them there. I was afraid that such a blockhead would drown them somewhere. It didn't help. They were already running to the boat. I promised to show them special devices I made myself, but they didn't even hear me. The boat was huffing, the bastard painted it red and made a mast, too, so the boat could serve as a lugger. Compared to mine, it looked like a ship or a yacht.

I pleaded with him to leave me alone to teach kids because saving human lives was important business. Even though he thought he was smart, I tried to prove to him that he wasn't. For this reason, I think, he and others who were there started to dislike me.

"How can you, old man, teach others when you've never pulled even a dead cat out of water?"

"So what if I haven't? I thank God for that. My beach is a safe one, unlike your graveyard."

"What do you mean 'my beach' when it belongs to the county?"

"You're in charge of it, so it's as good as yours. Just the way that this one is mine."

"Did you by any chance inherit it from your father?" he mocked me.

"I don't know about that," I said, "but I do know that my beach is safe and that at yours people flounder daily."

"Of course they flounder," he screamed. "But no one has drowned yet. There's not one son of a bitch who will drown while I am the guard. And you receive your paycheck for nothing. Since you've been employed, you haven't even gotten your nose wet."

This remark hurt me the most.

It wasn't my fault that people didn't drown themselves. I was glad. I'd rather be without a job than to see people drown.

This whole scene was happening right in front of my wife, Julienne. At that time I was already married with a baby on the way. She heard everything, and I saw that she was upset and even ashamed a little. Secretly she was looking around to see if anyone was seeing her humiliation.

"I showed him, didn't I?" I asked her later. She said nothing. She barely looked at me.

"I told him what's what."

Still nothing. Not even a peep.

"Why are you looking at me like that?"

"Who's looking at you?" she asked me. "Who could be looking at *you*?"

She went into the house, and I went after her. I wanted to clear up everything. I didn't want anyone to look at me like that. No one had the right to look at me that way. She, however, didn't say a word about anything, and I gave up.

"What kind of a man are you, Andrija?"

"What kind am I?"

"That's what you are—nothing. Everyone can walk over you."

"No one can step on me. Didn't you see the way I drove Zemba away?"

"You didn't drive him away. The man just left after he was done stomping on you."

"And what did you want me to do? To fight him?"

"You don't have to fight, but you shouldn't allow anyone to stomp on you like that."

I see what the matter is, but I cannot fight in the civil uniform. It wouldn't be right. It had just happened that the same month the county had given us new uniforms. They were green like nettle, and really unsuitable for work; the buttons were most annoying. I could never get comfortable with them. But, nevertheless, they were uniforms, a national emblem. It was a consolation at least not having to watch every other civil servant parading around in his uniform. Up until then, we were the only ones walking around half-naked like animals.

"I restrained myself because of the uniform," I said.

"You restrained yourself because you were afraid," she said. "You were shitting your pants."

I nearly hit her. I, scared? I would have jumped into the most perilous current had it been necessary. But I've never had to and that was not my fault. I didn't hit her, of course. It wouldn't be right to hit a pregnant woman and besides, I was wearing the uniform. Although it was not the army uniform, so it did not elicit the same respect, it was nevertheless a uniform, and it deserved at least a part of that respect. Besides, my Julienne was a strong woman. I'm afraid she wouldn't have gone down easily. Then there would have been a scandal, it would've spread all around the county, the supervisors would have found out, and I would've possibly lost my job.

What hit me the hardest was that after such altercations, Julienne would not let me come near her for weeks. Even then our love life was sporadic and irregular. You come home with the sun down, dead tired from observing and walking around—you say hi and she says hi. You're all worried, nothing is going on, the work is slow, and you need for someone to drown a little. Otherwise there goes the job, because why would they need a lifeguard without anything to guard, except to be a load on the budget? You ask for some food, there it is on the table, she says. You're good for nothing, you chew but you're constantly on edge because you think you're hearing a scream for help, though you know it's impossible because what fool would be swimming in the pitch dark, although there were a few, mostly bathing at the "wild beaches," which were not under my control. You ask for some wine, she says get it yourself, you ain't no priest. You undress quickly and fall into bed—good night, good night—you cannot wait to fall asleep so that the drowning men's screams would stop in your brain. I see that Julienne is drawing away from me. When I get closer, she pushes me away.

"This," she says, "is not advisable during pregnancy. It's not good for the kid. It could go deaf or something worse."

I, of course, do not force the issue—I'm not a pig. If the doctors don't allow it, then I won't fiddle with it. But I'm unhappy because I see we're drifting apart.

But going back to saving lives, I was more knowledgeable than anyone else in town. You can ask around. It was just that I was unlucky, and that was my downfall. You should've seen the gadgets and widgets I invented! *A double boat hook,* for example. In our job, as Zemba said before, the most dangerous thing is to get within arm's length of a victim. If you're in the water, he'll pull you down with him, and if you're in a boat, he'll tip you over. A victim is as good as an unconscious fool; you can count on him just as if he weren't there. But if you save him using my device, he can do you no harm. You throw a noose around his chest, just as if you were throwing bait, and then you reel in the line until it's tight, and since the device works as a fishing pole, you pull a victim out of water like a fish.

Dedicating my life to such endeavors, I, just like Socrates, neither had time to do something meaningful and worthwhile for the town nor for my house, meaning the boathouse, and lived my life in perpetual poverty. But this was all useless since in spite of my mental and physical aptitude, up to that point I had never saved anybody. *Ausser einem Hund,* except one dog, and, I might add, the dog was still a puppy. Someone had thrown it out into the river, so I saved it and adopted it.

God only knows how much I yearned for a chance to save someone. Anyone. Just to show that I was not getting paid for nothing.
That was the way I was: a good-natured man, *ein gutmütiger Kerl*.
You can ask around if you want. But the damned chance, however,
never arrived. The people, as if out of malice, always needed help on
the North Beach and never on mine, as if I were either damned or
as if my portion of the water, between the Bent Rock and the Great
Willow, were enchanted by some evil witch, so that anything baptized
that would go in must be spat out immediately. Zemba's region, from
the Great Willow all the way to the railroad station, on the other
hand, must have been destined to be like a sieve, letting everything
that moves fall into the river.

Please note that I did not wish any harm to any of my swimmers.
God no! What kind of a man would wish misfortunes upon others
. . . that people drown just like that . . . for my personal advancement
. . . or for my fame as a lifeguard. There were more important reasons
why I needed someone to drown. My raise, for example. This was
right before the war. Even though I was not paid much, we made ends
meet somehow. When my income was not enough, my wife worked
as a washerwoman around town. Otherwise, I didn't let her work. It
wasn't right for the wife of a civil servant to be a day laborer. On the
other hand, it was hard to live without her help. Inflation was high,
so every penny was needed. So that I would not have to listen to the
reproaches, I went to the county office, to personnel, to inquire into
things. I told them how things stood. I'm serving the king, wearing
the uniform of the kingdom, and my wife has to go door-to-door
looking for work. How can that be? They threw me out telling me
it wasn't their business. "Whose business is it then?" I asked. "The
county serves the town the same way that the government protects
the whole land. You must care about the government's employees."

"Go to hell, you fool," they said, and threw me out the door.

Considering it all, life was not so bad since I lived for free at the
boathouse. During the winter, in the off-season, the house was a bit
cramped, but in the summertime when all boats were out, we didn't
know what to do with so much space. At that time there were three of
us. My son Andrija, my namesake, was already born and at this time
was five years old. The war was not on yet, although everyone was
talking about its possibility. Mussolini had already invaded Abyssinia,

Selassie joined the League, Franco entered Madrid, Hitler marched into Austria, and the Jews marched out. Someone was always entering places and others were leaving. It was real mayhem all over the world. I was only scared that some Serbian lout would kill another Ferdinand so that we would have to roam among some big mountains again. All in all, it was bearable. Even had it been worse than that, somehow or other one had to keep a job. In such a crisis, I would not have been able to find another one.

Things were pretty bad at the beach, and the fact that I had no cases worried me more than a bit. I certainly wasn't paid per saved head—I didn't have some quota I had to meet, therefore I did not depend on traffic. I was on salary, so no matter what happened I was still getting money. What was disturbing me, however, was that no legal proclamation or law required every beach to have a lifeguard; it all depended on the county and how much sense and money they had at any given moment. I knew quite a few beaches around the county, some pretty nasty and dangerous, that did not have lifeguards at all. Everyone was saving bodies left and right, and sometimes they would just drown. In that respect, there was no order at all. Sometimes some neophyte would try to help, and he would either drown himself or drown the victim in the process. So, there were no regulations. Here in West Germany, there is one *Vorschrift* for everything; there is even more than one for the same thing. Only for bathing places there are three dozen of them, either regarding hygiene, *Sanitätsvorschriften*, or those regarding organization, behavior, and morals. In Serbia, you could even take care of your bodily needs and no one would say anything. You would just move away to avoid the smell. What I am trying to say is that if the county had been short of money, I would have been the first to go. They would send a commission, asking me how many heads I'd saved. I would have nothing to say to them. I could show them a dog, that's all; that was all I'd saved. They would fire me on the spot. I would have no place to go. And then, there was my family. Family in the house—a noose around your neck.

For all these reasons, I didn't dare to file a formal complaint against Zemba, even though he was mischievous, not out of malice or hate I think, but because he was that kind of a man. For sure I wrote many a complaint, but I never sent them. These grievances and reports were more like proofs to show Julienne that no one could tread over me.

However, I never sent them, but threw them into the river; as if the river could be of any help. In some way, perhaps it could have, if it had only enlivened just a little and done whatever the other rivers in the world do. I probably learned to write these kinds of statements at that time, and these, I think, have helped me convey a case clearly. So I sat down and wrote a grievance to the county president. It went something like this:

Article number one: Zemba, in an unfriendly and insolent manner, hinders my official duty; article number two: he plagues my customers and me with false alarms, and everyone well remembers the story about the boy who cried wolf; article number three: aforementioned Zemba uses a public boat for his personal use and enjoyment to boat around not only kids, which I do not object to at all, but all kinds of women and sluts, so that the whole beach reverberates with their squeals and squalls; article number four: even though paragraph upon paragraph specifically forbids gambling at public places, Zemba, in his boat house, which the county lets him use as his abode, brings various gamblers and all kinds of riffraff, and wastes the whole night playing cards and rolling dice so that in the morning he is practically good for nothing; what is worse, he does it right in front of the public, from which it could be conjectured that he does not object if his customers do the same. Therefore, considering all facts, his beach looks more like a midsummer fair or some Turkish brothel, except for racket and stalls or gypsy band, which would not surprise me if those appear sometime soon. This ruins the reputation of our profession, as well as of other government employees. Furthermore, Zemba, in his debauchery, goes so far as to extort money from those whom he saves, as if he were not already paid out of the county budget, and for this there is plenty of reliable evidence, but for now I am enclosing a list of names along with the professions of each ill-treated individual.

I more or less wrote in a similar fashion, but just before I licked the envelope, I paused and thought for a second: does Zemba really hinder my work, since I really haven't got any? His cowbell ringing irritates only me; no one else seems to even notice it, neither the swimmers nor the bathers; they just laugh about it. But this is the folk mentality. They are all soulless and without conscience. That's the reason things have not fared well, so far, for us. As far as gambling and whoring are concerned, who am I to judge? I myself didn't have the money to gamble and as to the other, even Julienne was too much for me. And in all honesty, my beachgoers behaved similarly to Zemba's. The willows were thick and people were bored. When the sun beats down on you and boils your brain, there's no way around it. As far as extorting money from people, it only shows, unfortunately for me, that he was saving lives, which I couldn't boast of for myself even if I'd wanted to. And besides, who could prevent people from being thankful? And so, whenever I would write the statement, I'd chuck it in the river. As if I was writing on water. It seems to me now that I've done the same thing throughout my life. I've been writing on water my whole life.

I wanted, more than anything else, to have a drowning case on my beach. Anyone would do. It could be a most ordinary—the smallest possible—member of the popular masses, as Comrade Ozren used to say. As unlucky as I was, I couldn't hope for a bank president. I would have thanked God for a clerk or even a night guard. A foreman would've been ideal, but I was in no position to choose, considering how low I had sunk, so I had to be grateful for anything the river would've given me. Most often, I hoped for a housewife. For example, she took a boat to market; a storm caught up with her on her way back; she knew how to swim, but that didn't matter when the waves were as big as a house; they tossed her overboard, and then I came just at the right time. I never hoped for a kid. Even though that was the likeliest possibility, I never wished for it even if I had to starve to death. Right away a picture of my son Andrija drowning would come up in front of my eyes. This happened only when, to my great consternation, I gave in and started imagining children drowning in water. He wasn't allowed to swim, so he sneaked out and jumped in the river as if tempted by the Devil. Luckily I was again in the right spot. In such deliriums I was always in the right spot. I swam toward the kid. When I get closer, I see Andrija's face. He's looking at me with his blue eyes as if to say: why me, Daddy? Since then I've never imagined a kid drowning again. I would rather die.

I admit, however, that due to privation, I started to eye the swimmers more frequently and imagined myself saving them, even though I was acquainted with them all really well and knew how little I could expect their help regarding my case. I could've done nothing about it. So I kept strolling down the beach, imagining my first save. Some days I'd stand back and just watch, just like a vampire, for God's sake. Sometimes besotted, I would start talking to myself, and people would say:

"Are you all right, Uncle Andre? You look a little dazed."

"Oh, it's nothing," I would say.

What could I have said? That I'm standing here waiting for you to drown yourselves? What would they think if they knew I was imagining their demise? And me, of all people, the one who was paid to keep them safe like you would a small drop of water in the desert. It's true what they say, that poverty and trouble could kill even the best of hearts.

Take Mr. Avakumović, the pharmacist, for example. A sluggish and hefty kind of guy, looking like a pudding all sprawled out on the sand. The water could have easily tricked him and carried him off. The trouble was he wouldn't swim. Not once. Not ever. He didn't even go as far as to wet his big toe, as if he were made out of sugar and was afraid of dissolving. All he would do was to sunbathe and pant in the heat, so his apprentice had to moisten him every once in a while.

"If you'd only jump in, Mr. Avakumović, you'd know what God's blessing is all about," I told him once.

"No way," he said. "It's not even an option."

"And why not?" I asked.

"I jumped once and barely saved my head."

"You don't say? And where was that?"

"In Novi Bečej, on the Tisza."

"Yes, the Tisza is a tricky river. You'd never guess that just by looking at it."

I was thinking to myself: Oh Andrija, my old man, where were you then when he was drowning in the Tisza?

"How'd you get out?" I asked.

"Some fisherman pulled me into his boat."

Of course, I was thinking, and that fisherman was not even a registered lifeguard. He was there by accident. Life's a bitch, as my friend Andraš used to say.

The wife of the judge, Mr. Veljković, was a perfect candidate as well. She was tall and skinny like a beam post, and looked as if tied up in hundreds of knots. She was always waving her arms and tripping over something. But as if out of malice, she was always either splashing on the sandbar or rising and falling, up to her belly, like a stork. I couldn't have gotten anything out of her unless she'd been sozzled or unconscious.

I didn't even look on Mr. Skrbinšek, a captain of the Second Regiment. He was the champion of his garrison in the style called front crawl. Soldiers in general, especially the young officers and petty officers—the old ones did not even come to the beach—I didn't even consider. They predominately swam in flocks. In such a crowd one could not drown unless he was a brick.

The experienced civilians I had to write off because of their technique, and the less experienced ones swam with the help of water wings, tires, and rubber apparatuses in various forms of animals.

I didn't count on families either. They entered the river in hordes, too, and once in they would incessantly call, count, and hail each other.

You could only expect something out of the ones who would come to the shore alone. The best time was before the high season. What made them wander around the beach by themselves, I couldn't say. Maybe they were considering suicide, or maybe they were like that by nature, eccentrics and loners. In any case, they were my favorites. I didn't take my eye off them. Secretly, of course. They're sitting on a rock and staring at the water; I do not move. I wait with a first aid kit ready to go. My double boat hook as well. I still haven't tested it in a real-life situation. All the while, I go over the whole procedure: Locate the victim. Swim evenly. Breathe rhythmically. Approach from behind. Grab the hair. Keep the head above the water. If needed, slap them across the face. After a while, the man stands up. I get up, too. Anything could happen. Maybe he's here to end it once and for all. If in fact he came for a swim—there were fools who would come around Christmastime and jump under the ice to retrieve a cross—there was always the possibility of a cramp due to the cold current. Unfortunately, nothing ever happened. The man would leave, and I, crestfallen, would go back to my boathouse.

Once, a man happened to be standing there, naked as a jaybird, with not a thing on his body except for a rubber swimming cap. I knew those showy bastards. They call them nudists. Here in West Germany they have them wholesale. They don't chase them away with sticks like in our country. Here, they collect them all in one place and fence them away from the honest folk. As for me, I used to chase them away from my beach. I had complete authority from the police to use any method, except to kill. But as soon as I saw the rubber cap, I knew what I had on my hands. Someone who wants to kill himself doesn't care about his hair. Besides who would want to drown naked? And these people don't just walk into the water; they jump in from the rocks. I also remembered reading somewhere about a doctor who killed himself by injecting morphine before he jumped in. He fell asleep among the waves and drowned peacefully. But nothing like that happened either. My nudist jumped in, splashed for a minute, and then walked out squeezing his swimming cap. Then I ran after him like a fiend and chased the maniac away.

Once I placed my hopes on a young man, a gentleman. You could see right away that there was nothing rosy in his life. He didn't look bankrupt since he was too young and green for it, and besides that, these people do not drown, but often either jump out their office window or run into exile. In this case, either a woman was involved or some terminal illness. All the same, this guy didn't attempt to take his clothes off. He just sat on the shore and stared at the waves. To be or not to be? He used to sit on the rock called the Curved Rock because it arched over a deep whirlpool. Every day he would get closer until he finally reached the edge, and from there you could go no farther but into the water. He had to decide soon, by the next day at the latest. I was so convinced he would jump that I thought I would start my motorboat early the next day, even before he showed up. So on the morrow he came again, dark faced like mire in autumn. I knew he was going to jump. It seemed there was so much darkness in his soul that I was tempted to hug him and take him home to pour our miseries out to one another. After that, let him jump. He wouldn't drown anyway since I would be there to save him.

I don't know what came over me. Something propelled me, either my goodness or the fear that he might drown—such eccentrics sometimes have miraculous strength—really I couldn't say what led me to waste such an opportunity. I walked over to him and said:

"Don't do it."

He turned his head in my direction as if he could only hear me and not actually see me.

"Who are you and don't do what?"

"Don't do whatever you intended to do."

"And what do I intend to do?"

"To plunge in."

"I didn't intend anything. Even if I had, it's none of your business," he said with a shiver and stepped closer to the edge.

I followed after him, step by step. "This," I said, "is my job."

All the while I was trying to dissuade him I was giving him the right to do it. I'm telling the truth. I thought to myself: really, Andrija, why are you meddling? Your job is to get him out of the water, not to prevent him from jumping in. This is God's will. However, I kept pleading and dissuading him not to jump. I asked myself whether to seize his hand or not. Finally, I grabbed it. He turned and pushed me away. I dropped on the rocks like a sack of potatoes. Later I fell ill from the fall. I could not urinate. My tract was all tied up in a knot.

"Go to hell, old man!" he said and left. I never saw him again except in the newspapers. There was his picture, and apparently a cable car ran him over. So there you have it.

■ □ ■ □ ■

CHAPTER THREE

YOU HAVE TO ADMIT THAT NOT ONE SERIOUS HUMAN PROFESSION CAN
sincerely be performed without its object. You can't be a doctor without patients nor a priest without a flock. Can you be a minister of
justice without injustice? Or a judge without a culprit? On the other
hand, I think, my destiny was commanded by God through prophe-
cies, through dreams and any other method possible. Therefore, it was
destined that I save people from the water. I have a diploma with all
necessary seals to prove this. Besides, I had an obligation to my father's memory. But to be a real lifeguard and not just on paper—forget about the uniform and authority—I needed a drowning victim.
And let it be known, I did not wish him to die—on the contrary, that
would have killed me right on the spot—but just to drown a little
until I got there to save him. But my river was cursed. I had a feeling
that even a rock wouldn't sink in it. My misfortune was getting to me
so much—I was getting really tempted to throw Shaban the Turk,
a nonswimmer who sold dates and baklava on the strand, into the
water—I even started to have dreams about it.

I dreamed of all sorts of things, all pertaining to water. The river
was always the same one, but it looked different from mine. It was
gray as ash. It flowed and dragged on forever, the current throwing
dead, drowned people onto the shore. It was as if you'd submerged
a doll, and, being light, it would pop right out of the water. Their
hair all raggedy, entangled, and entwined with mud and wattle; their
white shirts all in pieces, their nails sharp and broken—having grown

in the depths of the river—and their bodies all bloated and blue. They kept coming out and how many of them I couldn't say. They threatened me with their fists and cursed me for letting them drown. They wailed, but no sound came out of their mouths except for white froth, just like you'd see in a rabid dog.

In the beginning, on the first night, only one showed up in my dream: blond and hairy. He cries for help in his mute way: "Help!" I try to help him, but he's too far away. He's not even that far, but he keeps floating away from me. The faster I swim, the farther away he drifts. Then I notice that my legs are moving in circles as if I'm riding a bicycle, so there's no way I can catch him.

As time went by, they started coming to me in pairs, a male and a female, and after that all of them at once. As soon as I would try to save one of them, another would call me, and when I turn around to save him, a third one would jump out as if catapulted from a sling. The whole damned night I'd swim left and right. It was horrendous. It got so bad that I was afraid to go to bed.

Naturally, I stopped secretly eyeing swimmers right away. It didn't help. It looked as if the drowned had hooked themselves to the bottom of my soul. Something else helped, however. I started to get used to them. This didn't happen until the night their faces appeared. Up until then they'd been faceless, and instead had a blown-up muddle of blue painted clay. One night, I thought one of them looked somewhat familiar. A pudgy little man with a scar on his stomach. God almighty, I thought to myself, this is the pharmacist, Mr. Avakumović! How can that be if he never goes into the water? Maybe the river Tisza in which once he'd almost drowned spat him out? Maybe rivers keep a record of the people who've been saved? Who can fathom the secret of the waters? Afterward the wife of the judge appeared, Mrs. Veljković, floating like a plank from a wrecked ship, and even the judge himself appeared in his black robe. One after another, everyone familiar emerged: the gentlemen from the bank headed by the director Mr. Hadji-Simić, the doctor, Mrs. Marković, Shaban the Turk, and even that maniac with the rubber swimming cap. The gentlemen officers jumped out all together in one group, but what surprised me most was that the garrison crawl champion, Captain Skrbinšek, was amongst them as well.

As I said, from then on I was not scared anymore. In fact, I started to like my dreams. I could hardly wait to fall asleep because I knew

I'd be doing my job for which in reality there was no need. Although, truth be told, I have to admit that even in my dreams I didn't save anyone. I could never get close enough to the victims.

My duty suffered because of all my dreams. I was exhausted from swimming so much during the night that in the daytime, at work, I was always drowsy. I was practically good for nothing. This worried me. If something were really to happen, what would I do without my strength? Even a kid could've pulled me under. I was afraid to talk to Julienne about my dreams. She would've told me I was nuts. She might've even left me for good. Who wants to live with a loon! I was also afraid to go and see a doctor. What if they committed me? What would've happened to my position?

I decided to have a talk with Andraš. He was one with the water and knew everything about it. Even he himself, as he told me on numerous occasions, had nightmares, though not as horrible as mine. "In my sleep catched me a big fish," he used to tell me; he didn't speak Serbian very well, so he butchered sentences sometimes. "I can't get it out on dry land. I'm reeling like mad, the fish nothing. I keep it on, reeling; nothing. The fish swims away."

While all of this was happening, the Krauts had already waltzed into Serbia. I wasn't capable of fighting, and with all my dreams and misfortunes I was so muddleheaded I didn't even notice when they came in. Soon after, they rushed to my beach to swim. All of them tall and robust young men, real Goliaths. And such swimmers, too. Any stroke, any time. I wasn't going to have much business with them around. There was no way that they would drown easily. They fenced themselves off from the regular citizens. They kept me to take care of their part of the beach as well. That was where I learned some German, which came in handy when I got here. All things considered, it was the same as before the occupation. Nobody drowned, so I can't say I was any better off in that respect, and I didn't lose the chance to save people, so I can't say I was worse off than before, either. That was as far as I was concerned. Regarding the Krauts and them destroying my country, I was clean. I didn't care for those fiends and didn't do anything against the regulations. I consider myself a great patriot, even though it's been said I was a great traitor.

So one evening, right before dusk, I run into Andraš.

"*Jonapot,* Andrija," he says, which in Hungarian means something like good day.

"Hello, Andraš."

"How was today?" He would always ask me this first. He was a good man; as soon as he saw me, he would ask me about my day.

"Same as always," I say.

"*Nichts?*"

"*Ninch.* Nothing."

I'm waiting to bring up the subject. I'm feeling a little uncomfortable. He'll think I'm crazy. I'm leafing through the newspapers, waiting for a chance to bring up the subject of water. In the news, however, as if out of spite, nothing. Two victims of lightning in the mountains. A boy ended up under the trolley. Some guy grabbed a wet electrical cable and died. (At least this last one had something to do with water. The man was wet.) The guys in the forest blew up a locomotive. A hungry cat injured an old lady. Newborn puppies are always chucked into the water. But this was not a newspaper headline but a proverb. You can sense the way my brain was working at that time. Folk proverbs stuck in my brain, but only ones involving water. For example, he who comes in well, doesn't leave well; he who comes in guilty, doesn't leave alive. Or if the weather is bad, the travelers travel, which I understood as boats sail even in bad weather. If there's not enough milk, a river is always within a blink. Water and fire are good servants but bad masters. Water doesn't care about friendship. Water is no good even in a boot. Water carries away everything except for shame. Water and malice never go away, and so on and so forth.

But the damned newspaper has nothing about water. A little girl died in fire. Hostages executed. Explosion at a retirement home.

"Nothing," I say.

"What do you mean nothing when the German troops march into Kiev?"

"God willing, they'll all drown themselves," I say. "But let me ask you something Andraš. Do you have dreams?"

"What kind?"

"Horrible ones."

"You dream ugly?"

"Well, I can't say they're ugly. They're not ugly to me, except that my dreams force me to swim all night long, so in the morning, during work, I'm good for nothing. Do you see how deep I've sunk?"

Then I tell him everything from the beginning to end. How at first I was afraid of my drowners, but now I'm so close with the dead that I can't wait to see them again every evening. He shakes his head and says: "It's no good. *Ninch.* Not good at all."

"I see that."

"You, Andrija, no like your customers."

I am panic-stricken. "Of course I do. Do you think I'd be a lifeguard if I didn't?"

"Why you wish then for your swimmers to drown?"

"Who says I do?"

"Dreams. You dream what you wish."

I start thinking that maybe he is right. Maybe I really do. Maybe not for them to completely drown, but only a little, just enough for me to come and save them. Because a death at my beach would be more painful and disgraceful than the lack of a saved life.

"What should I do, Andraš?"

"I haven't a clue."

"What do you think if I go see a priest?"

"What priest has to do with it?"

"To say a prayer for me and chase the spell away."

Andraš did not believe that was a good option. How would I explain to the priest what I wanted? He thought that nothing could help me until I had my first save.

To foreshadow things to come, I have to say he was right. The dreams stopped as soon as I had my first case. My misfortunes, which came afterward, were much greater, but they are a different story.

The dreams, damn them all, kept coming but in reality nothing happened. On the other hand, I thought, as is well known to people, slow running water can erode a mountain. I was hoping that with time I would get better. I was particularly counting on the beginning of the new season. Every season brought a new generation of young and inexperienced swimmers, and even the old ones at times would be still rusty and need to thaw themselves from the wintry frost. The water was still pretty cold, the currents strong, the weather unpredictable, gales menacing, cramps always possible, and so forth. Anything could happen. But, as always, nothing did. Partisans mined the railroad bridge, so the Germans established a curfew, so everyone had to be either home by seven or possess an *Ausweis*. But an *Ausweis* was hard to come by, so who would have one for swimming? The beaches, therefore, were out of the question.

Andraš often stopped by to inquire.

"How was today?"

"Same as always," I answer. "Same as always."

"*Ninch.*"

"*Ninch.* Nothing. And how could it be otherwise when they prohibited swimming? On the other beaches, however, a true apocalypse."

I'm showing the newspaper to him with the most important headlines circled. Deadly jump in the river for one hundred dinars. A fisherman dies after his boat overturns. A man falls into deep water and drowns. A seventeen-year-old journeyman disappears in the river. Water washes up an unknown body. Saving each other, two brothers drown themselves. Just in one spot two of them.

"No worry. Just wait and watch," says Andraš. "A drowning will come. Just like come fish. I spread my net and sit and wait. The fish come when I least expect."

"It doesn't work, Andraš. I have no luck. It's better for me to leave than for them to fire me."

"When the curfew stops, it could get better."

It was the same. The curfew was over, the beach got livelier, but still nothing happened. Andraš had an explanation even for that.

"The reason is the season. Maybe season is wrong. Like in fish. There're good and there're bad seasons. This bad season. Next much better. Someone will drown."

"Listen," I say. "I don't even want people to drown on my beach."

"I don't say you want it. All I say it is good for business. No catch any fish, you no fisherman. What's fisherman without fish?"

"He could still be a fisherman. A fisherman with no luck. Just like my father. A fisherman without a catch. In any case, I've been thinking."

"It's no good to think."

"I'll grow old without having accomplished anything. When my grandchildren ask me what did you do, Grandpa, all your life, what will I tell them? I waited for someone to drown? What kind of job is that, they may ask? You see, kids, I waited to help people. So did you help them, Grandpa? I didn't. No? And why not? Nobody drowned. Nobody needed my help.

"You see, Andraš, after a while the shaft that keeps a man together cracks. He can't go any longer. It went as far as it could. The axle is broken. I've decided to leave my job."

"You can't do that," he remonstrates. "You can't abandon the beach in midseason."

"This is no beach!" I continue my rant. "This is no river! This is a puddle, Andraš. Soon frog spittle will appear. And then, what kind of a job will this be? I'm sitting on the beach, waiting for someone to get in trouble. And I'm not only waiting but wishing it, too. Where's the sense in it all?"

"Every job is like that: scabby. No doctor until someone sick. No gravedigger until someone die, no soldier without war, nor a lawyer without someone gets in jail. That's the way it is in this shitty life."

"That's what I say. Why should I depend on misfortune? I'm not the kind of man to live on someone's misery."

"And what are you gonna live on?"

"Something will turn up. I'll go see my mother," I say. She was still alive at that time.

"It's a good thing," he says, "that your mother has no river."

"Who says there's no river there?"

"I been there."

"There's no river, that's true, but there is a lake."

"When I been there, I see no lake."

"Back then, there wasn't one," I explain. "But the government fixed up the power station. They brought water, flooded the mine. Because of rain, because of underground water, the lake appeared. They named it the Yell Lake. When you shout, the rocks echo your voice."

"Lake don't move. No danger of drowning, and no need for a guard. What would you do there?"

"Up to now it hasn't moved, but you never know. There's still the underground water, and they're at work. One day it's gonna be a hell of a lake. If God only sends some rain and a flood or two . . ."

"You crazy? What flood?" he yells.

"A small one. Very small one, enough to liven it up a little."

"So would that make any difference in your life?"

"Listen, Andraš!" I yell. "Are you my friend?"

"Of course."

"Then shut up."

However, something kept me there. Somehow at that same time, crimes against the masses became more frequent. Dead bodies started to float down the river. It was driving me insane. With the first few, I made a mistake. I saw something dark in the bushes, so I thought to myself: maybe someone drowned in spite of me being there. That would've finished me on the spot. Only when I pulled the man out, I saw he was butchered like a chicken. The weight went off my shoulders. I reported the case thinking it was some score settling, when at the county office they started to cuss and howl. They said to watch out and let them know because "damned be those Reds, there's going to be more of this." And there was. That summer I pulled out so many bodies, I couldn't count them all. Even my double boat hook was finally put to work. But the reason I'm mentioning this actually has to do with another dreadful event. Soon after, due to the epidemic, they banned swimming. So from a lifeguard I went to being a gravedigger.

The decree was issued and delivered to me in the morning. And this happened around three in the afternoon, around dinnertime. I had not even fully evacuated the beach, when two men showed up at my door. One of them was wearing glasses and the other, without glasses, had a tiny mustache like Hitler. "We're from the municipality," they said. "Inspection."

I'm screwed, I thought to myself. What can I do? It's been bound to happen sooner or later. It lasted long enough. Jump in and float away, Andrija. You decided to leave the post anyway. But it's one thing when a man leaves on his own and quite another when he's fired.

"Are you the keeper here?" asked four-eyes.

"I am sir," I said, without mentioning my lifeguard duty.

"What's your name?"

"Andrija Gavrilović."

"What is your middle initial?"

"A, sir, for Andrija."

"You're pretty stingy with the names around here, aren't you?"

I saw their type right away: a Scrooge and the Devil. There'll be trouble, I thought. But you, four-eyes, you're not going to screw me.

I said, "That's the way it is when you're poor."

"OK, Andrija A. Gavrilović. How long have you been here?"

"Forever."

"What do you mean—forever?"

"Well, since it opened. Fifteen years."

"A long time," said the Hitler with the mustache.

"To me it's not a long time. When you do your job faithfully, there's always something to do. Clean up this, fix that. This thing over there needs fastening, this one over here unfastening. You know how it is. This is water—a natural element."

I was speaking clearly, I knew, but as to what I was saying—I had no idea. All the time I was trying to avoid mentioning lifesaving. Regarding everything else, maintenance, sanitary regulations and laws, I had no fear. In that respect I was clear. I forgot about leaving the service. I felt I'd brought all this upon myself for cussing out the river. While the fiend in the glasses was leafing through some forms and applications, I swore to myself that if I got through their fingers unscathed, I would never say one word about leaving my post again. If I could only fool them now, I thought, I'd live to see my retirement here. What else do I need? I don't care about lifesaving or whether I have any victims or not. I felt as if a veil had been lifted from my eyes. What a fool I'd been! Instead of being happy that I was getting paid for doing nothing, I worried myself to death. I suddenly realized that it was even better if I had no cases at all. At my age, who would want to get wet, especially since I had already caught rheumatism?

"It's stated here that you are paid to save lives, too," said four-eyes.

I'm dead, I thought.

"I am, sir. I have a diploma for it."

"And how many times have you had to intervene?"

"The gentleman means how many boats and cabins I've fixed?"

"What cabins? I'm talking about lives."

"Well, now, you see," I tried to drag on, "this is a safe bathing place, people are water-savvy, then you have curfews and the latest epidemic, the work is short, and I'm here all the time to remind them to keep safe."

"How many then?"

"None," I muttered and closed my eyes.

"What?"

I opened my eyes. They couldn't believe it.

"What are you trying to say?"

"That I've never pulled anyone out of the water."

"Why for God's sake?"

"It wasn't necessary, sir. Nobody was drowning."

"No one has drowned in fifteen years?"

"No one."

"And all this time, you've been getting paid?"

"Yes, but the pay is close to nothing."

"Even the smallest pay amounts to a lot if you're getting paid for doing nothing," said the one with the glasses. Hitler was silent, as if he were more understanding.

"What can I do?" I tried to defend myself. "It's not my fault, gentleman. The river is like that. And then the partisans are blowing up one thing after another. Now there is this bloody epidemic. Everything has gone to hell. But if you allow swimming and bathing again, I hope . . ."

"What are you hoping for, Gavrilović?" the one with glasses continued to drill me. "You hope that people will drown?"

"No, sir, I'm not an animal. I just hope that in case I am needed, I would be able to show myself in a real light. And where the river is concerned, one never knows what to expect. Do you understand?"

"We understand," said Hitler, looking uncomfortable. "We understand everything. But you need to understand us, too. Don't think we don't appreciate your zeal, your effort, and your overall competency. Even your peculiar inventing ability." (I had shown them my double boat hook.)

"Make sure you patent all your inventions, so you don't get robbed," said four-eyes. "There's no doubt that you would be on top of things if the opportunity were to present itself. But neither you nor anyone else wishes for that opportunity. The beach is safe, and the river is quiet. At this time, even swimming is prohibited. No one knows how long this may last. On top of that, there's no money. Every penny is worth saving. You see for yourself what times we live in."

"Are you firing me?"

"Yes," said four-eyes firmly. "Why wiggle around the point? There's no budget for you."

"The refugees are eating the whole thing," said the one with the mustache.

I started to drown. I asked, "Who will take care of the beach and the inventory?"

"The guard from northern beach can take care of the southern one, too," said the mustache. "We're sorry."

"No worries," I said, but in reality I was drowning inside. "I have a diploma. There will always be work for me." But I thought otherwise. I knew everything was over.

Suddenly the bell sounded. Everything echoed and reverberated as if laughing at me: let's go, Andrija, go to work, Andrija, a life is in question. I didn't move 'cause I knew it wasn't real. This is all Zemba's doing, I thought. Even if it's not him personally, he's afraid of the inspectors, so he sent someone else.

"What is this clamor?" asked the inspectors.

"Nothing," I said. "Zemba is fucking with me."

"Someone's drowning!" they hollered and ran outside.

"This cannot happen here," I said and followed them slowly without hoping for anything. "Even a brick wouldn't drown in this water."

But as soon as I had gone out, a chill ran up and down my spine. It was Andraš who was banging on the bell. He was banging and yelling:

"There's a kid in the water! A kid in the water!"

"Is this for real? So there is a God after all."

"What are you waiting for, you idiot!" the inspectors yelled. "The kid will drown."

As if paralyzed, I couldn't move an inch. In my mind I kept visualizing my Andrija, but he was right next to me. I got so anxious, I didn't even notice him there. Some red fog seemed to have enveloped me, and I felt a burning sensation all over. My head felt empty, like a grave before a funeral; all I could feel was heat and sparks. Finally somehow I came to my senses. I ran back to the boathouse, grabbed the first aid kit, and then ran back outside. I remembered my double boat hook, so I dashed back inside for it and then continued to the river. As I was running, I was trying to undress, but those damned buttons . . . I knew they were trouble. I tore them off. I kept tripping over the pole. I can't tell you if I fell over it or not. I don't remember it well. All I can say is that the boat wouldn't start right away. The cord was red-hot, but the engine didn't want to turn over. The inspectors were running amok as if crazy. They stopped yelling by now, but their mouths gaped open. Andrija, in an attempt to help, was running ahead of me, pointing his hand toward the water.

I couldn't see anything—that's how scared I was. I beg you to understand, this was my first case. And right in front of the inspectors as if I were taking an exam. Right then and there, I understood everything clearly: if I save the kid in one piece, they'd rescind the firing. Nobody would have a heart to fire a lifeguard. Even if they did fire me—the government sometimes has no soul—I would have reasons for an appeal.

Luckily, the motor started. At the same time I comprehended the whole situation. It was Kole, a kid I'd taught how to swim. He was a good swimmer, so seeing him there surprised me. I thought it was a cramp or a strong current. In a moment I got near him. The water was carrying him straight toward me. It couldn't be any better.

And then it happened. If I live one hundred years, I'll never forget it. I was just about ready to throw the hook—I saw that miraculously Kole was conscious and even extended his arms to me—when the fucking wire wrapped around my legs. That's the truth. The wire from my double boat hook enveloped my ankle, and I dropped headlong straight into the water. And it wouldn't have been so bad—from the shore it might've looked as if I jumped in on purpose—but I hit my head on the edge of the fucking boat. I was knocked out and had no idea what happened afterward.

They told me later that if it weren't for the kid, I would've drowned myself. He pulled me out. A drowning person saved the lifeguard; this has never happened before in the whole wide world. At least I could say I was the first to do something. They fired me on the spot. I had nothing to say in my defense. It was stated in the notice: "due to fatal incompetence at work."

However, they let me continue living at the boathouse for a while. Because of the kid, I assume. Fair enough. They said, "If you'd have saved the victim, it would've been a different story. This way, we're sorry." I shouldn't have used my hook, not for any reason, until I'd perfected it. But I wanted to show off in front of the government inspectors, and I sure did.

Also I have to add that as soon as I got fired, Zemba's conduct toward me changed fundamentally. Whether he felt sorry—he didn't know that things would go that far—or guilty, I don't know, but he told me, as far as he was concerned not to hurry with moving out. We could've stayed until the county kicked us out. I think that deep down he wasn't a bad fellow, perhaps a little flighty, and that half the time he did not mean what he said.

While I was in distress, he said:

"Collect yourself, Andrija. It's not your fault. Your invention is as good as God given, but those shitty gentlemen from the county have never in their life had to deal with people drowning, so they don't know what kind of scum we have to deal with on a daily basis."

"Don't talk like that, Zemba. They are unfortunate souls."

"Unfortunate souls, my ass! They would squeeze the last drop of water out of a dry bone. All they do is wait to grab you and then drown you. Later they pretend to thank you. And some of them don't even do that. As soon as they catch their breath, they start hating you as if you personally forced them into the water."

"They are probably embarrassed to be an inconvenience to you."

"They don't give a shit about me. They don't even ask me for my name. And when I meet them on the street, they turn their backs like I was contagious. I've had enough of them."

"And I believe that each one would be dear to me like a brother. I think that afterward I wouldn't let him out of my sight. The life is in question. Somehow we would be connected."

"A good story," said Andraš. "Like in church."

"What's next? Am I supposed to support them financially? Leave them my inheritance?" said Zemba.

"I don't know," I said. "I didn't have a case, so I can't categorically say what I would do. I would take care of them somehow."

"You had the case," said Andraš, "but not luck."

"And I thank you for that. You tried to help me, but when you're jinxed, nothing can help you."

"Nothing I did for you," declined Andraš.

Then I explained to him that I had heard from Kole how he was not really drowning—there was no way that such a swimmer could—but when the inspectors showed up, Andraš coaxed him into pretending, so it would look like I was rescuing him. But even that wasn't the truth. Andraš related it to me once Zemba had left. He was apparently afraid to tell me in Zemba's presence because Zemba had forbidden him to do it. This was all Zemba's idea. Kole and Andraš just executed it. So there you have it. You see now what kind of people we are.

That was the way it all happened.

Then I decided to move out of town to a village. Even Julienne herself realized that we couldn't stay anymore. We began to prepare for the move. The season was coming up—there is nothing to say about the winter—they allowed swimming again, and the first people were expected at any time. I didn't have the guts to show my face in front of them, stripped of uniform and brought so low. And I was already afraid that the shame had spread all over the county. Just what kind of a man they've had for a lifeguard all these years. You could feel at this time the warmth of the sun on your skin, and the water was getting warmer and livelier. The sand at the beach was starting to melt, and the days were getting longer. Everything was in bloom. Summer was approaching, but not for me.

And then, suddenly, everything got turned upside down. I'm going to write the explication about that now because this event was the root cause of my misery and my subsequent collaboration.

■ □ ■ □ ■

CHAPTER FOUR

THE EVENING BEFORE THE MOVE, I WAS IN A LOAD OF MISERY. ON THE next day I was supposed to say good-bye to the beach where I had spent fifteen years of my life. I'd become bound to that merciless river like a man who in the end coalesces with any calamity. The two become so inseparable that the man stops noticing it. I knew the depths of her soul. According to whether she was rustling, purring, murmuring, grumbling, or roaring, I could always tell her mood. Every whirlpool, every curve and willow bush, every sandbar, and every current and depth ten kilometers upstream and downstream of the cabin was known to me. The beaches I don't even want to mention. I could recognize every stone and tell you where it came from. And now we were parting, most likely, forever.

After dinner I started on my last walkabout. It was warm outside, the beginning of July. The moonlight twinkled and shone like mercury. What magnificence! All around except inside of me. It's hard to describe that feeling. Just like when they tell you to go into retirement, and on the last day while you are packing, the janitor cleans around your belongings, raising the dust, and you know you're nothing to him anymore. I touched and bid farewell to every tree. Under my fingers, on the tree trunks, I felt incisions made with a knife. Normally I would have been angry with those who engraved their names and all kinds of lewd expressions into tree trunks and the walls of the cabins—I was always at war with them. As if by miracle, I noticed I wasn't thinking the way I used to. These people must have experienced something wonderful if they'd decided to remember it forever, if only as an engraving in a tree.

I can't say why I pulled out my penknife and started etching my name in big Cyrillic letters. ANDRIJA A. GAVRILOVIĆ, THE SOUTH BEACH LIFEGUARD. That was what I intended to write. I thought I'd say FOREVER, but I wasn't sure. Also I wasn't content with the years. You know, from–to. I was still alive. On the other hand, it felt as if I wasn't. I could easily say that 1944 was the year of my death. The moment I stopped working, I was dead.

I was engraving the letter *G* of my last name when I heard someone calling from the water. The words were indiscernible as if gurgling full of water. I quivered as if gripped by an electrical current. A drowning victim, no doubt about it, because no one else could make such sounds. You only babble like that when the aquatic claw grips your throat. Even though I didn't have enough luck to hear these sounds as a lifeguard, I've remembered them since my childhood, and later on I heard them in my dreams. The dead souls in hell must moan like this.

I ran up the Bent Rock and right away I saw what the problem was. In the middle of the river a current had seized a boat, whirling it like a whiplash. About ten meters away, a man was trying to swim toward it. Considering that the boat was not overturned, I concluded that the man was one of those eccentrics—I've already mentioned them before—who like to swim in the river naked. He went out himself in the dark, probably didn't want to have problems with the authorities; the moonlight tricked him, he jumped, swam, underestimated the distance, and then cramps caught him and turned him into stone.

I rushed to undress. All of a sudden, I heard a reproachful voice in my head, but it felt as if it were coming from the side.

"What's going on Andrija? What are you trying to do? You're not employed anymore."

"But I'm still human, though."

I continued undressing, but the voice was unrelenting. It kept bothering me.

"Stay put, Andrija. Let them see what it means to be without a lifeguard and what a horrible blunder they made when they fired you."

"Let the man drown so I could get my job back?" I was approaching halfway to the scene of the accident. "Besides they may reactivate me after this. It's no joke to save someone during the night, and all that without being employed. Finally this would be my first case. Any way you look at it, this is what I've been waiting for my whole life."

I plopped into the river, forgetting all the rules. I was dazed, the cold water grasped me, and my heart nearly came to a halt. It sucked me in at first and then threw me up onto the wave. It handled me like I was going to drown. Normally, in these cases, the water will let you take two deep breaths before it pulls you under. Luckily, I recovered my senses and loosened my arms. I started to swim toward the victim now, properly and according to the rules. If someone had been watching, he would've had something to see. But as my luck would have it, no one was there. Even what was happening to me now, after so much time of wasteful surveillance, had to happen secretly without a witness at an ungodly hour, instead of in the daytime in front of a large crowd. As if drowning was a shameful ordeal and trying to save the person something even more despicable.

The poor victim seemed voiceless. Only an imperceptible murmur was coming from his throat. He stopped resisting. He must have realized he was done for. "Hold on, I'm coming!" He sank. Where are you going now, I thought. Don't disappear on me now. Then he emerged a little farther down. He fluttered with his hands and vanished again. The third time he tried, but I snatched him by the hair. You're mine now. Thank God, he was completely unconscious; otherwise, I would have had to smack him Zemba-style. Within me no strength was left, as in a child.

In this way, gentlemen comrades, the water and I had finally gone head to head, and I won. You can imagine how proud I was for saving this life. Finally I could say I had a reason for living. I know it is not humane to talk in this way, but I am narrating how it was and you can be the judge.

I pulled the man out onto the dry land. He was naturally heavy, but bloated with water he was even heavier. I barely got him out. Immediately I did what I was supposed to do. I was scared to death that he would die, that I would lose him now after so much grief and hard labor. Only after I was certain he was breathing, did I hurl him on my back and carry him straight to my home.

"What is that? Who is he?" asked my wife, frightened.

"Don't ask!" I couldn't catch my breath. "Help me!"

"Tell me who this is."

"I don't know. The victim. Hold his legs."

"What are we gonna do with him?"

"Put him in bed. What else?"

"Covered with mud like this?"

"Hold his legs, God damn it!" I yelled. Julienne realized the full gravity of the situation. She's never seen me this way, so she helped me lug the body across the room.

"Take it easy," I grumbled. "He's not a trunk."

We placed him onto the bed and wrapped him with blankets to warm up. Julienne started to heat up some milk. I sent Andrija to town to fetch the doctor and began to massage the victim. I rubbed his chest, squeezed his limbs, and blew my breath into him.

"You know what?"

"What?"

"What would you think about lying down next to him?"

"What are you saying?" She looked at me as if I were mad.

"To warm him up a bit, otherwise who knows what could happen."

She didn't answer, just crossed herself three times.

Finally I was able to calm him down. He started to breathe more regularly and his skin returned to normal color. For the first time all night I was able to take a good look at him. He was a robust man, white skinned but all flushed from vigorous rubbing. His hair was silky blond and thin, and his mustache had a white tone to it.

"An ugly sort of man," said Julienne.

"I don't think so," I disagreed.

"As if you know what's ugly and what's not?"

"I know a handsome man when I see one."

"This one isn't, for sure. He looks like Joško, the butcher."

"You don't know what you're jabbering about."

I was insulted, as if she was comparing me personally to Joško. But now, while I am writing this explication, I realize that my victim was probably not some great beauty. I, after all, didn't say that, but to me, while I was watching over him and counting his breaths, he appeared like a white chubby cherub who, with wet wings, had emerged from the water.

"I haven't seen a prettier drowning man."

"Of course you haven't since there weren't any others."

"I can't stop looking at him."

"Since you're cracked in the head."

"How old do you think he is?"

"How would I know?"

"I wouldn't give him more than forty. He's barely thirty-five. Do you think he has any kids?"

"I have no idea, and besides, why does it matter?"

"A strong man like this must have at least three kids. Do you think he has three? Two for sure. One boy and one girl."

"Sure, and their names are Milan and Milena."

"How do you know? Do you recognize him?" I asked. I was so agitated that each word was catching me like a fishhook.

"If you can guess that he has a boy and a girl, then I can imagine their names."

"This is no joking matter, Julienne. Don't mock. And as far as his children, I didn't guess. It's a custom with gentlemen to have a boy and a girl. There's no money or time for more."

"And you already know that he's a gentleman."

"An important one. I can tell by his hands. He must be some kind of appellate judge."

"Why an appellate judge?"

"No reason, but it would be nice."

"It would be better if he's a businessman," said the always pragmatic Julienne. "It wouldn't matter that he's a judge since they have nothing to eat either."

"Maybe he is a businessman. Nowadays only businessmen are this plump. Surely he's a businessman. A wholesaler."

"A colonial importer, I bet."

I didn't care that my wife was mocking me. I was dreaming.

"His parents are probably still alive. They don't even know that their only son almost drowned."

"Now, he's the only son, too!"

"When there are twelve of them, nobody notices that one is missing."

"You, Andrija, are a great fool," said my wife.

"Let me be one, I don't care, as long as he keeps breathing."

As if out of spite, he started to gasp for air and then his breath was gone. Agony. Misery. I jumped on top of him with all my might. "Don't do this to me now. You can't die on me now. It's not fair, it's not humane to die on me now."

Even my wife was distressed. "He's gonna die! What are we gonna do?"

"Pray, for God's sake, kneel down and pray!"

She actually knelt down. She was out of her wits, too, and me along with her. I didn't pray as much, as I was terrified. Only nasty oaths and curses were on my mind.

Just as quickly as it started, the agony ended. His throat cleared as if the wind was blowing through it. He started to breathe quietly again and the color returned to his cheeks.

"It's over," I said.

"Is he dead?"

"I wish you were dead!" I howled at her. I did not know what I was saying.

She, of course, got insulted. "You can't talk to me like that." To pacify her, I started to relay to her my expectation. "The river has finally shown her true colors. Although for now, only at night. But . . . she's been dormant for years as if enchanted. Now she awoke, changed her temper. It is the same with people. The most dangerous ones are those silent types when they're provoked. And with our river this is only the beginning. When she comes to her senses and collects herself, she'll create wonders. And when accidents occur frequently, there must be a lifeguard to prevent them. And where is he then? He's not here. Then one must be hired. And who's most responsible for this beach? Who knows her best? Who snatched a drowning man from her clutches? Andrija A. Gavrilović. He even has lifeguard certification. So where is this Andrija A. Gavrilović? He's not here. He was fired. He was fired as incompetent for service. What do you mean incompetent when he saved a life? And at night, no less? Saved a man from the furious waves."

"There were no waves," said the wife.

"I know," I said. "It's figuratively speaking."

At that moment, outside on the gravel, tires screeched to a stop. We heard voices, commanding in German. Commotion.

"My God, Andrija!" screamed my wife. "What have you done?"

"What have I done? I rescued a man."

"Not a man, Andrija. You've saved a partisan."

"What're you talking about, for God's sake?"

This can't be true, I thought to myself. It's not fair. My first case— and he's from the forest, too. It didn't make any sense, either. What would a partisan be doing in the water? Who would be in the mood for swimming when they're used to being chased like mad dogs? I looked at the man on the bed. He wasn't white anymore but appeared black as the darkest devil.

Helmeted German soldiers with pointed guns burst through the door, and among them was our doctor holding my Andrija by the hand. His pajamas stuck out under his coat, and on his feet he had slippers. He was shaking terribly, and I barely heard his voice when he said:

"Where is he?"

I showed him. I tried to get closer (even if he was a partisan, he was still my case), but the soldiers pushed me into a corner. "*Vorwärts! Vorwärts!*" It was useless to explain. At that time I didn't know the language as I do now. I knew a word or two, but I understood quite a bit.

The doctor leaned over the bed and felt the victim's pulse.

"*Er ist ausser Gefahr, meine Herren,*" he said, which meant that the man was saved. "*Er ist eben wieder zu sich gekommen.*"

The Germans roared. At that point it became clear to me that this fellow was not some partisan (thank God), but belonged to the Germans, either a soldier or an officer, but most likely an officer, because otherwise they wouldn't have bothered so much. Not until they picked him up in a blanket did I say anything.

"Where are you taking him?"

The doctor stepped closer, took his glasses off and asked me:

"Do you know who this is?"

"No," I answered. "Who?"

"Kreiskommandant, Standartenführer SS, Erich von Rüchter."

"That's nice," I said. "I didn't know that. He was the same to me as any other drowning person."

I'm drawing your attention to his conversation, which our doctor, if he's still alive, can confirm, because it's evident that I didn't know who I was saving out of the water, especially that he was ranked so high.

"There are people, and then there are 'people,'" said the doctor dispiritedly.

"That may be so, but the water doesn't choose. It doesn't care about friendships and status."

That's what I said with a clear conscience. I would've been happier if he was our man, if a Serb had been drowning, whether he was a judge or not. But as I'd said, the water doesn't choose, nor does a lifeguard. If that was not the case, do you think that Dr. Karamazović, who was a great patriot and saintly patron, would have treated such a man as the *Kreiskommandant*? All right, it could be argued that our Mr. Doctor was forced out of his bed in slippers and a nightgown, where I voluntarily pulled our enemy out of the water. That's true, but also our saintly patron Mr. Doctor could have refused to treat the enemy. He could've, he wasn't a mute. He could've said: "Kill me but I don't treat the aggressors." Mr. Doctor—Julienne would be able to confirm this—he rushed over here. Why, I ask you? Some might say out of fear. And I say it wasn't fear but his medical conscience and his ethics. His ethics forced him to rush over.

I saw the soldiers circling around my man. They're gonna take him away from me for sure, I thought. I didn't know if I was going to see him ever again. Soldiers are nomads. They often get transferred elsewhere in a second. Or they get killed. At that time, in the woods and pretty much everywhere else, guns were firing all the time. Nobody knew who was shooting at whom.

"Over my dead body," I said and told them that I wanted to go with them.

"Why would we need you?" said the doctor confrontationally. He was a little feisty, as if I had saved a dragon, and now he had to take care of it.

"I want to retrieve my blanket."

"They'll send it back to you."

"And I want to look after . . ."

"Look after who?"

"What do you mean who?" I said. "The victim."

"And what do you think I do?" exploded the doctor, and he shoved me out of the way of the car where I had been standing while they were taking care of the victim. Then he yelled at the driver:

"*Los! Fahren sie! Schnell! Schnell!*"

And then they took him away. They kidnapped him. And we neither looked each other in the eyes nor shook each other's hand. He didn't even thank me. Zemba's words came to my mind. "As soon as they catch their breath, they look at you as if you personally forced them into the water, and the next day, when you meet them in the street, they turn their backs on you."

Is that possible? I thought. Could it be that no one would hear about me risking my life and putting my family and myself in peril? Could it be possible that everything would vanish like writing on water?

"Nobody will know about this, my friend Andrija," called the same voice that had tried to prevent me from jumping into the river. Apparently I was not employed, was not authorized, was not called for.

"And why would no one hear about it?" I asked.

"What do you think, you idiot? Do you believe they'll accept the fact that a *Kreiskommandant* almost drowned?"

"Why wouldn't they? It's not a disgrace. It's a tragedy."

"For one of our men that would be a tragedy. For a German officer this is an embarrassment. Especially that a Serb saved him."

"When I jumped in the water, I was not a Serb but a lifeguard. And he was not a German but a man in trouble."

"True. While he was drowning, he was just a person and nothing else. But before and after that—*Kreiskommandant* and a German SS officer. They are slaughtering us like pigs, and we are saving their lives."

"So," I thought to myself, "they might not give me my job back?"

"Of course they can do that. They can do whatever they please, Andrija. They might think you'd begin bragging about how you dragged one of their officers naked out of the river, so in order to shut your mouth, they could throw you straight into a concentration camp. You and your wife!"

"I'm not going to tell anything to anyone dead or alive."

"They don't know that."

"Of course," I thought. "They can't know that."

"And you, be honest now, would you be able to keep quiet and say nothing to anybody?"

"I can't say that I could. I'd probably explode."

"There you have it then. And what's one or two more to them?"

"That's true. What's one or two more to them?" I said out loud.

Then my wife woke up and shrieked: "Get up! Are you off your rocker? What are you jabbering about?"

"Pack our stuff, and don't ask any questions," I told her.

"You just said earlier to unpack everything."

"Now I'm telling you to pack up!"

"But why, for the love of God?"

I told her quickly. She understood everything right away. When evil is in question, man doesn't need too many words to understand everything.

"Where are we gonna go?" she wailed. "Where in the middle of the night?"

"I don't know yet. I just know that we need to get out of here. We can't be found here in the morning."

"We're not going anywhere," she said suddenly and fell on her knees and burst into tears. "Look!"

I looked through the window and saw a car driving along the gravel toward the house. It was the same one that took my case away.

"You and your river," she kept crying. "You can both go to hell!"

I was close to crying myself. One time I save someone, and he'll cost me my head. Even though he didn't hurt me then, as I thought he would, still the way things have worked out, it would've been better for me and my family if that night my ears had been plugged with wax. Because if I hadn't heard the cry for help and had not saved that Erich, there would have been neither my collaboration nor exile and the subsequent murder of which I am convicted.

Two soldiers in uniform and one in civilian clothes stormed into the house. The latter one was our man, a collaborator and real shit, as Comrade Ozren likes to say.

"I am," he said, "the translator for Kreiskommandatur. Get ready and come with us."

"Where are you taking him?" asked my wife. They said nothing at first and just kept rushing me on.

"He'll see," said the translator finally.

I was so out of my wits that I didn't even say good-bye to my family or tie my shoes. I remember that I was only shifting some strings and some odds and ends from one pocket to another while muttering something all the while. Julienne later told me that I kept repeating: "Why me? Oh God, why me?"

They drove me away to Kreiskommandatur, led me through numerous tunnels—I've never seen so many tunnels all at once except here in Munich's jail—pushed me through some thick doors and locked me in.

The room was tiny, a real shoebox. You could hardly breathe inside. No windows. There was a hole, probably used to be a chimney, and even that was screened off. The walls were painted white. As for the furniture, there was a *Schreibtisch* and two chairs, one without a backrest. The lamplight was roasting my brain, and on the wall, just ahead of me, hung a picture of their hunchbacked Hitler with the following words written underneath: EIN VOLK, EIN REICH, EIN FÜHRER.

I sat in the chair without the backrest. I didn't want to make them mad right away because I figured the other chair was for someone more important. I started to think about my current situation. That it was a good one, I could not claim. What kind of good could you expect out of Fascist scum? So the situation was bad. According to their *Vorschrift,* they'd taken me in for questioning, and then, as I thought, it would be straight to the camp. And I want it to be known that those *Vorschrifts,* or regulations, are still the same. Here in Munich, too, they questioned me constantly—I was sick of questions—and then they sent me to jail. They could've done this immediately. Why waste time? The Kreiskommandatur could've sent me straight to the camp, too, but they followed the regulations. A German wouldn't go against the regulations even if you threatened to kill him.

I couldn't think of anything clever to say. I'm no Socrates. It looked to me as if I was trying to scoop water with a sieve. Who'd have believed me if I'd told them I wouldn't talk? If I told them I was leaving town, they could say, "You'll talk wherever you go." I was only hoping to beg them to leave my wife alone. Andrija was a child; he wouldn't have remembered anything. I was hoping they would show that much humanity.

After half an hour, the translator showed up along with another officer.

"This is Herr Hauptmann Frost. He is going to question you now, so you'd better watch out what you say."

"What can I say," I asked, "when I know nothing about anything?"

I said this by accident because I didn't know what else to say. As soon as I'd said this, I realized that it would be better if I kept a crumb between my teeth or, to be clearer, took the oars in my own hands. What did I have to lose? Could things get any worse? And this way, with some luck, I could get through with only a few smacks on my hand.

"*Wei heist du?*" asked the officer. The translator translated and I understood some as well.

"Andrija A. Gavrilović, Herr Hauptmann."

"*So.*"

He offered me a cigarette just like Comrade Ozren does now. I took it. It could've been my last one, I didn't know.

"You are the lifeguard?"

"I was, Herr Hauptmann, until I was fired."

"*So. Und warum hat man sie entlassen?*"

I told them because there were no cases; nobody was drowning.

"So? And why, *warum*, were there none?"

"The water was that way, Herr Hauptmann. It was more like a puddle full of crap than a river."

"Listen, you donkey!" yelled out the translator. "German officers cannot drown in shit puddles."

"I didn't say they do." I was guiding the water toward my own mill.

"*Was sagt er?*"

"*Gar nicht,* Herr Hauptmann!" answered the translator, thus saving me from possible wrath.

"*Heute nacht,*" asked the officer, Herr Hauptmann, as they called him, "*du warst also nicht im Dienst?*" He wanted to know if I'd been working the night before.

"*Nein,* Herr Hauptmann."

"*So? Und was, zum Teufel, hast du mitten in der Nacht am Ufer gemacht?*"

"And what the Devil were you doing there in the night?" translated our man.

I answered that I was just walking around, getting some fresh air. "*Ich bin spazierengegangen.*"

"*Luft schnappen,*" explained the translator.

"*So. Und was geschah dann?*" "And then what happened?"

I hardened my soul, and, even though Mr. Kreiskommandant had become dear to me as my first case, I threw him back into the water.

"Nothing," I answered. "Nothing happened. After I was done walking, I came back home."

"What are you talking about, man!" shouted the translator.

"I'm telling you what happened."

"What about Herr Standartenführer?"

"What Führer?"

"The colonel you saved out of the water, you idiot! Mr. Erich von Rüchter?"

"I didn't save anybody. I have no idea what you're talking about."

"*Was hat er gesagt?*" asked the captain.

The translator started and then stopped translating as if he didn't know what to say. Look at him, the ragamuffin, writhing there, I thought for no reason. This was the only thing the Kraut wanted to hear anyway.

"Listen, Gavrilović," started the translator again. "I'm scared to translate what you told me. I told him you're still confused and can't remember everything yet. I told him you're still in shock . . . now, pull yourself together; I'm telling you this for your own good. Just tell him how you saved the man, because if you're evading the question, he might think that you're collaborating with the partisans. You can't play with this guy. He's worse than the plague."

All the while Frost kept repeating: "*Was hat er gesagt? Was hat er gesagt?*"

"I have nothing to tell him." The partisans didn't scare me. The Krauts know I have nothing to do with those guys. But I don't want to expose the colonel, the SS *standartenführer,* to any gossipy rumors.

"I'm telling you, man to man, to stop this foolishness."

"I'm not fooling around. I'm telling the truth. I didn't save anyone. Not in my lifetime. I've never seen a person drowning, and what's more I've never saved one. That's the way the water is here. A rock could swim in it."

"*Was sagt er?*"

And slowly, stuttering, he translated everything word for word. Not a nerve on the captain's face moved. He didn't twitch. He just sat there, staring at me. I thought he was going to say his "So," possibly offer me another cigarette and then send me back home to continue working as a lifeguard. He did in fact say, "So," but instead of everything else, he leaned over the desk, didn't even leave his seat, and whacked me across the face, completely smashing my cigarette.

With me, this business with cigarettes has always been a weird one. I don't remember finishing even one like a real man. Someone always either knocks it out of my mouth or engages me in conversation so that I forget to inhale, and after a while the cigarette burns out. And no one ever gave me one out of sheer goodness. I was always asked to work for it. Kulman used to give or take cigarettes according to the circumstances noted in the explications. Comrade Ozren, however, never snatched any from me. Only once, when I made him extra mad for not helping the country receive the war reparations, he snatched a pack of cigarettes from my hands and stomped it to pieces. "If I could, I would do the same thing with you," he said.

The slap on the face completely dazed me so that I turned to the translator and asked him in German:

"*Was sagt er?*"

Amid all the anguish, he smiled.

"If it wasn't you, then who saved the *standartenführer*?"

"I didn't know he was drowning."

"You knew very well, but you're pretending. I just can't figure out why or what for."

I know why, I said to myself, but instead I told them:

"If he was drowning, it must've been someone else who saved him, so you better go and look for that person. You can tell Mr. Captain that I'll never admit anything even if he beats the living Jesus out of me."

And they did, gentlemen comrades. They surely did.

What they've done to me since the death of my benefactor, Geheimer Kommerzienrat Herr Gruber, was nothing compared to what Herr Hauptmann did. Here in the beginning, they slapped me and punched me a little, but quickly and on the sly. One of those devils stepped on my foot so savagely that I limped for weeks. They told me that was private and not official. *Entschuldigen Sie bitte.* They told me I would get compensation. *Entschädigung.* All that was nothing compared to Frost and his methods. But I endured. I did not say one word about my case. I had only a hard time with urination, but I had this problem ever since the suicidal case when I fell on the rock doing my duty as a lifeguard. I kept denying everything Herr Hauptmann asked me. It helped that I knew they were not beating me for real, because even though I was taking a beating and a pretty good one, too, they weren't doing it out of hate but out of necessity. They wanted to be convinced that I would not say anything. I kept telling myself, hang on a little longer, Andrija, just two or three hits, and then they'll let you go home. They might even get you some cigarettes, *entschuldigen Sie bitte,* and reinstate your position at the beach. So.

I didn't crack even when they brought a doctor to examine me for insanity. *Entschuldigen Sie bitte,* "I don't know anything, and I didn't save anyone."

They stopped as suddenly as they started. They washed me and combed my hair. You couldn't tell I'd been beaten at all. They were real experts. I thought now they would give me some cigarettes, then *entschuldigen Sie bitte,* then pack me into the car, and send me home.

But this didn't happen. The door opened, and who do you think stood there? It was my case in a uniform. He was all shining as if bathed in Sidol. A smell of cologne filled the room, and medals hung on his lapel. He started to shake my hand, smiling all the while. What could I do? How could I deprive my first case from shaking my hand? It crossed my mind that they were trying to test me, but it was too late. I was already smiling, shaking his hand and asking about his health. The translator was working hard to keep up. You could tell he felt relieved.

How is Mr. Colonel? Did the water cause him a lot of harm? Did I hurt him during the save? I tried my best—I know my duty—but you can never guarantee in such haste and even during the night. And with the waves like mountains, we both barely survived. Thank God for moonlight because without it, it would've been mighty bad. Was everything all right? *Entschuldigen Sie bitte.* And so on and so forth. I could not stop blabbering. I was working like a turbine.

He, on the other hand, kept saying:

"*Gut, gut! Nur keine Aufregung! Es ist alles gut, es ist alles in bester Ordnung!*"

OK, I said to myself, as long as everything is in *Ordnung;* I don't care what happens to me now.

What followed was like a dream.

As soon as the colonel left, everyone swarmed around me. All of a sudden, everyone behaved differently. They offered me cigarettes again. I took every one of them and put them aside. I didn't know when someone might rip one out of my mouth. Everyone was jumping around me as if I were a brazen chief. That beast Frost was the most animated of them all. He was apologizing for something the whole time. "*Das Missverständnis,*" he said; it was a misunderstanding. "*Entschuldigen Sie bitte.*" All right, I thought. Just keep those fists away from me. I swear, I'll remember them as long as I live. In the meantime, they gave me a close shave, dressed me in a black suit, put brand-new shoes on my feet. They said that no one could go to an *Empfang* in rags. After all was said and done, I looked like some big-shot official. I didn't even look that smart on my wedding day. Then, you won't believe it, they put powder and makeup on me. "What are you people doing? I'm no homo to paint myself." It was a necessity according to my translator. "The newspaper will be there. They'll take a picture of you, so we must do it to put some blood into your cheeks." "Well, you didn't have to drive it out of my cheeks." He said it was my fault, that I was stubborn as a donkey. He kept asking me why I was denying and holding up everything, and why did I not tell the truth in the first place.

"I don't know why. Just because."

"It can't be just because."

"Well I didn't want to praise myself."

"So, out of modesty?"

"Yes, out of modesty."

"You aren't all together, that's for sure."

Again they led me through some hallways and tunnels, and everything was fine. Please come this way, please come that way. *Hier entlang bitte, hier hinein bitte. Bitte links, bitte reshts.* We came to some door as big as a church entry. A soldier who stood in front clicked one heel against the other and said sharply: "*Ihren Hut bitte!*"

I gave him my hat; it wasn't mine anyway. I didn't know what was going to happen next. In the movies I had seen folks leaving their hats before entering a hall, but there were normally people dancing inside. I couldn't dance even one step and had never done it in my entire life. Not even a *kolo*.* And then again, it was not a suitable place for it either. This was no church portal set up for a wedding. This was the Kreiskommandatur.

Inside, it was swarming like a beehive. There were so many people I couldn't say who was who. The room opened up from one end to another like the Vatican church and was jam-packed with serried civilians and people in uniforms. There were mostly Germans, but also some of our people as well. SNG, I thought, the Serbian National Guard, which belonged to Mr. General Milan Nedić, the late Ger-

---

* A folk dance performed, ideally in a circle, by a group of people holding one another either by the hands or around the waist. The word "kolo" means circle.

man collaborator. In the crowd I recognized the mayor and a few other high officials. Everyone was applauding. I was walking and they were applauding. I inquired of the translator the reason for all this. "This is for you," he said. "Why me? Who am I to deserve this?" "A hero. You're a hero." He shoved a glass in my hand and led me toward my case, who was holding a similar glass. In fact, everyone was holding glasses. The alcohol was flowing in gallons.

In all honesty, I can only recall the beginning of this fiesta, and what followed I can barely remember. Everyone was drinking fiendishly. I was unaccustomed to cognac, especially on an empty stomach, had barely slept in days, and considering the beating I had taken, everything was muddled in my head. I have no recollection as to how I ended up back in my house, passed out in bed. I shall relate only what I can recall, but for the cussing and for the unpatriotic behavior I beg forgiveness on account of the alcohol and the general confusion caused by the events and my first case.

Mr. Colonel raised his glass and gave a speech. I will quote it verbatim from the newspaper. Besides the diploma, the newspaper article was the only other document I carried with me into exile. Here it is:

"Ladies and gentlemen, I raise this glass in honor of the victorious and mighty German Reich and its leader Adolf Hitler, and my savior Mr. Andreas Gavrilović, and to honor the friendship between our two nations! I trust, ladies and gentlemen, that it will meet with your approval when I say that the action performed by this good and valorous man cannot only be attributed to a mere act of humanity, and even less as an act executed out of an official line of duty, since he was off duty at the time, but as another public expression of appreciation that the citizens of this town have toward the victorious German nation, its leader, and its glorious army."

All the while I was thinking to myself, I have to be thankful to you for drowning yourself, and I won't be able to repay you for the rest of my life. I was probably mumbling something because the translator asked me if anything was the matter or if I had something against the speech. "No, nothing's the matter," I said. I told him that everything was all right as long as they weren't beating on me, and then I proceeded to tell him about my lifelong gratitude. That bastard, as soon as he heard this, translated everything word for word. People applauded again. Some of them were even taking notes in notebooks. I wished Andraš were there to see me then.

The colonel continued his speech and the translator continued to interpret:

"Now you must realize, gentlemen, that I was right in asserting that we do not understand these people at all and that we judged them with prejudice. It is a mistake to judge the whole nation according to the actions of a few fanatical Bolshevik bandits! We must view them through their authentic specimens, among which my savior, Mr. Andreas Gavrilović, undoubtedly belongs. And I am confident, ladies and gentlemen, that while he was rescuing me, he did not perceive me as an ordinary individual in dire straits but as a symbol of the German nation, its power, and its worldly mission, although considering his lack of necessary education, he wouldn't be able to express his feelings eloquently enough with words."

I quickly added: "I did it more out of conscience."

Mr. Colonel replied: "*Typisch slawisch, diese Formulierung!*" and continued to speak, but I really couldn't remember what about. The alcohol was already getting to me, and I started to lose it a little. There's nothing about this in the newspaper; there's only the beginning of the speech, but if you are interested, you could ask the town mayor about it, if he's still alive.

I only remember that after the words were over, the colonel started to walk around the room. This worried me a little, so I followed along. He led the way, I after him, and after me the translator with a bottle. I did not let my case out of my sight. I was worrying. He was talking too much to my own liking. After a person almost drowns, he must lie down to prevent the body from a relapse.

"This is bad business," I said to the translator. "His lungs are still weak. After so much water, everything is washed out inside and thin as paper. Look, he doesn't shut up, just talks and talks."

The translator said nothing, but instead shoved another glass into my hands.

"He's a smart man. He should know he must take care of himself. What's the point of me rescuing him if he dies now?"

"Drink!" said the translator.

"Why don't you tell him to shut up?"

"Just drink, old man, and don't worry. This guy's strong as a buffalo."

"No one is strong in the eyes of water. Compared to it, we are this small."

Then I clearly remembered that we were photographed. First it was me by myself, then the case by himself, and then the two of us together, like brothers, in various poses. There was one where we were hugging each other, one where we were shaking hands, one with me toasting with my glass, and another with him toasting with his, and all these were either from afar or up close, from the side and from the front. I've never been photographed so much in my entire life. I barely made it. And while we were posing like that everyone was yelling, "Come on Andrija, say something! Why don't you say something?"

"What do you want me to say?"

"Anything!"

"Ask me anything, and I'll answer."

Right away, one of them with a camera around his neck asked me how long I'd been a lifeguard or something like that—I don't remember exactly—and I thought this was a good opportunity to say what had been bothering me for a while:

"I was, but I'm not anymore. They fired me for incompetence, fatal incompetence. It was the inspection. One of them with glasses and another with a mustache. I have everything written down on paper. I've had no cases, and on top of that this world crisis. The budgets cut down to minimum, and refugees everywhere like grasshoppers. Corpses are floating down the river. The public beaches are shut down. Contagious infection, they say. What infection? Since when is butchering infectious? This is not cholera, gentlemen. Then, they threw me out on the street. After so many years and with a diploma hanging on the wall. I even had a uniform with brass buttons. Just like a general. Everyone respected me. All I had to do was to show up. *Ordnung* must exist. It must treat everyone equally. No discrimination. I cared neither for fathers nor for uncles. So. But what can you do? Until I saved Mr. Colonel, I had no cases. Tragedy. As if the invasion wasn't enough . . ."

"Drink, Andrija," coaxed my translator.

"And the years were passing. Nothing was happening. Zemba had three cases per month. Directors of the credit bureaus. Wholesale dealers. Each a high-ranked gentleman. I even wrote petitions. It didn't help. You see the situation for yourself. Dreams completely crushed me. I used to struggle with vampires throughout the whole night. And during the day I was eyeing the swimmers. To get my first case, I was close to pushing somebody, some domestic imp who . . ."

"Drink, Andrija!"

"I had my eye on Shaban the Turk. Do you know Shaban? Baklava and dates. I figured he was a Turk, so what the hell. If I'd rescued him, he would've been a Turk again. Drowned and dead in water, he's neither a Christian nor a wholesale dealer. Nothing. I couldn't count on that. Hands get out of shape and the brain stops working on the same wavelength. Everything in a lifeguard gets out of tune. The inspectors fired me for Kole's case. You know Kole? One with glasses came. A real snake. A Fascist . . ."

"Drink, Andrija, Mr. Colonel will get insulted," the translator kept pressing me, doubled over with laughter.

I didn't refuse. "Anything for Mr. Colonel. Even though it's well known what he is. But a lifeguard is like a doctor. He even has to treat a skunk . . ."

"You were talking about the inspectors," the translator returned me to the previous subject.

"I know. You don't have to tell me. I've had it up to here. But I had a misfortune. A string wrapped around my legs. I even invented it. Of course, inventions always trick their inventors. It had a double hook, too. It worked on a principle similar to . . . it wasn't meant to be, gentlemen. They gave me a slip. After fifteen years in the government service and with a diploma hanging on my wall."

"You can write down, gentlemen," the translator interrupted me, "that Mr. Andrija Gavrilović, by the explicit order from Colonel von Rüchter, will be reinstated into service."

Only then did I notice that everyone around me was writing and photographing everything, so I fired up to explain everything, especially to the one who had come from Belgrade and whom they introduced to me as Fedor Negovan. Right away I asked if he was any relation to the builder, Mr. Constantine Negovan, for whom I used to work before I devoted my life to the rescue business.

"I am."

"How's the old man?"

"Good," he said. "He's dead."

"How could that be good, by God? What happened?"

"He fell into a lime pit."

"If I'd been there . . ." I started, but the translator stopped me.

"Better tell us how you did your job."

"How I did my job? I didn't. How could I do it without any cases? And the damned string wrapped around my feet. Then there's no money. Invasion. Fucking corpses. Our troops are retreating everywhere. One misfortune after another. Misfortune was after me even while I was working for the deceased boss Constantine. Bricks were always falling on my foot. What a man he was! There are none like that nowadays. Worked with us the whole time. Drank a gallon a day and cursed the gods . . ."

"Drink, Andrija!"

"Cases were nowhere to be found. There can't be a doctor without a patient, Andraš used to say. Do you know Andraš from the river? Neither can there be a gravedigger without a dead body. And he must take care of himself. He'll catch pneumonia, and then what do we do? I was a gravedigger during the typhus . . . it was hitting the lungs like a drill. It kept boring and boring. *Z-z-z-z-z-z* . . . Come on, pour it in, a rescue doesn't happen every day. Mr. Colonel broke my jinx. Now I hope it'll get better. There're so many Krauts on the beach . . ."

A coughing fit seized the translator.

"But I'm not that kind of a man. I'm not a mean person. I could've rescued even a drowning Serb if I wanted to. One of them I prevented from jumping. So I wasn't only looking after myself. As a result of a fall, my bladder got tied up in a knot. And the streetcar driver didn't care, did not come down to stop him. Didn't give a damn. He trampled everything he could find like a German tank. People are scum. And we call this Serbia? This is not Serbia; this is a whorehouse, gentlemen . . ."

"What happened with the dreams?" asked the translator.

"I got used to them. So. Especially because the next day I would meet them all on the beach. The same ones, all alive and healthy. People even drown in lime pits. The pit is two by two, and they still manage to drown, but in my river nobody. Is this fair, gentlemen? 'Scuse me? Just ask, I'll tell everything . . ."

The journalists inquired, and I gave them smart responses. My head was getting muddled since I was not used to the drink, but I held on somehow, weighing every word.

"Even though I was fired, gentlemen, I still felt responsible for that beach, unlike our ministers who fled while the people were drowning. A uniform doesn't constitute a humane service, gentlemen. It's true that I was watching even at night. There are idiots who swim at night. Of course I didn't mean to include Mr. Colonel in the same group. They say he wasn't only swimming but observing, too. I don't mean to go into that. Did I hear a gunshot? No, I didn't hear a gunshot. (This about a gunshot didn't make it into the newspaper report for some reason.) I only heard Herr Oberst calling for help. *Ganz so.* Yes, I intervened immediately. No, I wasn't afraid. It's my job, *nicht war?* Water is my element just as war is the colonel's element. I was only afraid for him, if he was gonna hold up until I arrived. *Jawohl,* there were waves. *Nein,* they weren't overwhelming. Approximately between half a meter and less. No, there was no storm, but the current is strong there and it's very deep. *Sehr gefährlich.* Yes, Herr Oberst conducted himself really well. Good swimming technique, you could tell. *Nein,* he wasn't unconscious. He was completely aware even though he lacked self-awareness. He was a great help during the rescue. It was a great struggle, *meine Herren.* The elements and a Serb. Aquatic body versus human body. Was he wounded? No, he wasn't wounded. (They did not put this into the report, either.) *Jawohl,* gentlemen, *nein,* gentlemen, *jawohl, nein . . .*"

Now I need to correct something for which I apologize profusely. Old age has caught up with me, and my memory is abandoning me. Only in the beginning did I answer so nicely. My rambling about the work, typhus, my invention, and the Fascists came later on. I see now that had it not been for the translator, I would have dug myself into a deep hole. Maybe I would have even ended up in a concentration camp. He saved me with constant interruptions and coughing. But, on the other hand, it was his fault that I descended into such a driveling state. He was constantly refilling my glass, urging me to drink. I wasn't used to it, and that was it. But everything I said only exposes my soul and testifies that I am a patriot and not a shit and a wicked collaborator. You can ask everyone who was present at the ball, if they're still alive, because all of them were shits and traitors.

At last, I finally lost it. I got so smashed that I didn't know who I was. *Wie ein Schwein!* I awoke in my bed the next day and heard from Julienne that they dumped me out of a car onto the gravel like a sack of potatoes.

And who would not have gotten sozzled, gentlemen comrades? I have to admit that I was happy that day. Without exaggerating too much, this might have been one of the happiest days in my life, but this was not hard to imagine, considering that my life had never been flooded with them. I must say, I would have been happier if I had rescued one of our own men, especially a partisan (unless he was either a bombardier or a dynamiter—those guys were sucking my blood; because of them the beach would shut down three times a year), even if he was not as eminent as Colonel von Rüchter. According to Comrade Ozren, the colonel was so famous that his name was even mentioned in the Nuremberg trial book, albeit in small letters. I hope this is clear. I was in no position to choose. This wasn't a marketplace where everything was out in front of you on a counter and you could just select what you wanted. Neither could a doctor choose his patient nor a gravedigger his corpse. Similarly, I couldn't pick whom to rescue. I want this one, but that one is out of the question. How would that look? A lifeguard, even if he wanted, has no time to deliberate. He jumps first, and then later discovers why. This way I could even pull out the Devil by his horns, a long-tailed fiend. Would I be guilty then? For this reason, my rescuing a Kraut was just a case and nothing else. A shitty one, no doubt about it, considering that for four years they'd been screwing us . . . even shittier considering that it caused me to be labeled as a collaborator and a national traitor.

Socrates talks about all this with much more eloquence. If you don't believe me, look it up for yourself. At least you can pick up a book and read it, since everyone else here has refused. They all said it was not applicable to the trial case. That was Dr. Hamm. Dr. Kulman told me that I should have read it before I committed the murder because now I can forget about it. Comrade Ozren didn't say anything. He just asked me if Socrates was some emigrant, and if so, where he lived.

But here is what Socrates the Greek says regarding his and my situation:

"Citizens of Athens, this is truly how things stand: whenever a man places himself, believing it to be the best place, or wherever he has been placed by his leader, there he must stay, as I think, and run any risk there is, considering neither death nor anything else, before disgrace . . . Then, gentlemen of Athens, I should have been acting horribly, if, where God posted me, as I thought and believed, I feared either death or anything else, and deserted my post."

In my case this means that I had to jump into the water and rescue the man when I was called upon to do it, instead of choosing when and when not to perform my job.

Furthermore, Socrates says: "But I showed them again, not with words but with actions, that I, if this is not too coarse to say, feared no death at all and that my only concern was not to do anything either iniquitous or blasphemous."

So it was with me as well. And you will be the judge.

And regarding the fact that I did not go to the woods and fight, which was never a part of the charge, although it did surface during the trial. For example, "So you could serve the Krauts, but not the people." I, by the way, did serve the people, although not all at once but individually, depending on how much trouble there was at the river. That there was no need for me to do anything, that was not my fault. The water was at fault.

As far as the accusation that I was talking favorably about Germans, I can say that I did not. I did as much as Socrates had. In this regard he says: "I call many of you to be my witnesses, and I beg you to inform each other and say how many of you have heard my conversations. There are many of you like that. Report, therefore, to each other, if any of you have heard, either a little or a lot, me talking about such sub-jects." You can inquire about me from Andraš, and from Zemba, and from many others in the town. I hated the Krauts as much as the plague. But only while they were in uniform. When they would come to my beach to swim and sunbathe, I could not say I hated them even if I stood in front of a firing squad. How can I hate a swimmer if he's under my care? So some have probably heard me talking in such manner about Colonel von Rüchter and quickly concluded: "This man has sunk low; he loved the Germans." I did say good things about the colonel, but for me he was not a German. For me he was my first and only case. To blaspheme against him would be to blaspheme against a gift from God.

So much about Socrates and myself.

■ □ ■ □ ■

CHAPTER FIVE

THE NEXT MORNING AT DAWN I WOKE UP AND RUSHED TO THE TRAIN station. The newspapers used to arrive from Belgrade by train, and you can understand that, considering my state, I couldn't wait until they distributed the newspapers to kiosks and tobacco stores. I wanted immediately to see what was written about me.

At the station, dogs were blocking the entrance. I knew most of the workers there, mainly from the beach where I often let them cut in line to use the cabins, and now they were telling me, "No way. Wait in line like everyone else." I tried to explain, but it was useless. However, they were reading the paper themselves, guzzling moonshine during work, leafing through the pages, and whispering furtively to each other. I begged them at least to tell me if they had anything for me. They refused even that. "Go to the store," they said with a frown. "Get lost! Don't you see we're busy?" And the whole time they were chugging the bottle and jabbering about politics. That was their whole business. The animals!

"All right," I said. "You come to my river. And then we'll see."

"I'd rather swim in shit!" one of them yelled.

I made note of him and headed to the store. I could hardly wait for them to open so I could buy the paper. The *New Times* was its name. It had four huge pages except during the religious holidays. In my distraught state, I had a hard time holding them. There was nothing on the first page, just as I expected. I read through it anyway, just so I wouldn't miss anything. With the news, you can never tell. They know how to situate even the most important thing so that you can never find it unless you read everything line by line. Supposedly they did this not to alarm anyone, which was all right, but no one was going to pull the wool over my eyes.

MINISTER GOEBBELS ABOUT THE INEVITABILITY OF THIS WAR. Blah-blah.

MUSSOLINI'S DECLARATION TO ALL ITALIANS.

GERMAN-ROMANIAN TROOPS CONTINUE TO ADVANCE TOWARD THE NORTHWEST OF IASI. I thought this headline would have been great if this was the year 1941 and the war had started in Romania. Under the current circumstances, it failed to impress.

THE BOLSHEVIKS EXECUTE TWO HUNDRED UKRAINIANS. God rest their souls, but we were missing a few as well.

ON THE WAY TO THE FINAL VICTORY. Ha-ha.

WESTERN INVASION ENCOUNTERS STRONG RESISTANCE.

PRIME MINISTER NEDIĆ CONCERNING THE INVASION. Why does he need to be involved in everything? I thought. There's no reason for us to be a seasoning in every European hodgepodge.

FINAL RESULTS OF THE ELECTION IN IRELAND. (I've always voted for the radicals, except for once.)

VICTOR EMMANUEL ABDICATES. *Auf Wiedersehen!*

GENERAL ALEXANDER SABOTAGING THE DEFENSE OF ROME. All nonsense.

The second page was even worse:

Invasion commanded by Moscow, barbarians in Rome, the Anglo-Americans are playing their last card—as if the war was a card game—Marshal Pétain's appeal to the French people, the question of to be or not to be in Europe, they are never going to get through, Stalin censors Churchill's last speech, von Weizsäker to keep his post, French indignant toward the invaders, the victims of the Anglo-American terror, "we shall endure and win in the end," said the leader of the Reich, multitudinous parachute troops mostly destroyed, fierce battles around the city of Bahia—nothing about me!

I was panic-stricken. Especially since there was nothing on the third page either. Only some gibberish about the black market, about the forest bandits, about the consequences of the Easter bombing of Belgrade, about some international glass shortage, about arrests, trifles and trivialities. Nothing but mere trifles and trivialities. Not even a word about me. Those fucking Fascists, I thought. They'll see if I save another one of them. Their mothers didn't teach them gratitude.

Not until the fourth page did I see it. The article took up the whole page: SERBIAN CITIZEN SAVES A GERMAN OFFICER. The picture was almost the size of my head. That was the major one, and there were some smaller ones, too. It was blurred a little but recognizable. Underneath it said: THE MAN WHO SAVED STANDARTENFÜHRER SS ERICH VON RÜCHTER—MR. ANDRIJA GAVRILOVIĆ, THE LIFEGUARD AT THE SOUTH BEACH IN THE TOWN OF G.

Mister! Mr. Lifeguard! Andrija Gavrilović, Mr. Lifeguard who saved Colonel von Rüchter. A mist gathered in my eyes, and I could barely read the letters. Where is my mother to see me now? But Andraš, Zemba, and Julienne will see it. And even my little Andrija. The whole town will have to accept me. I don't need a monument; just human acknowledgment, that they know who's who.

Then a crazy idea enveloped me, from which you could best tell my state of mind. What if I'm only in this paper and the other copies don't even mention me? Instead of me, again the black market, invasion, killing of the Ukrainians, and the international glass shortage. I knew, of course, that there existed a Belgrade edition and one for the interior of the country, and that because of our proximity to the capital, we received the Belgrade edition. I thought that I would not be mentioned in the edition for the interior, as if I was not as important for the rest of the country as much as I was for Belgrade and its vicinity. This was a reasonable idea, but to doubt that instead of appearing in every copy of the Belgrade edition, I would be in every tenth or even twentieth copy, this shows I was completely out of my mind. I went back and bought ten additional copies. I sat on the sidewalk and opened every copy while people stared at me. And lo and behold, I was in all of them. Of course. And pictures, too. One big one and several small ones. Me and the case. Only me. The case alone. The two of us shaking hands. Then the one where he was toasting me and vice versa. Depending on the print, in some I looked better than in others. In all of them, however, I looked waxen. From the makeup, I reckon. I shouldn't have let them do it. But who asked?

I ran home. I hoped the wife would be happy. A part of my reputation was surely going to reflect on her as well. It was no joke to be the lawful wife of someone whose picture appeared in the newspapers. Suddenly you find yourself among the ministers and prelates. And once you're thrown into newspapers, then it becomes easy; they just keep reprinting you over and over. That at least is what I've concluded. The pictures are always the same. A man gets old, but pictures never do. You die at eighty, but your picture shows you when you were twenty, so someone could think you died at twenty. This is the custom. As I was hurrying back I thought, you'll see, Julienne, no longer can people reprove you for being the wife of that blockhead Andrija who passes as a lifeguard but has never saved even one human life. They'll have to say, "Julienne, who is married to the one who saved the German Colonel von Rüchter, the one whose picture keeps appearing in the newspaper."

I kept running, and then stopped. I couldn't wait any longer. I flashed over the text: unselfishly risking . . . a victim of infuriating waves . . . after a long and desperate . . . his bravery . . . I couldn't make any sense of it. I couldn't calm down.

I started to yell even before I stepped through the door:

"Serbian citizen rescues German officer."

She was silent.

"Did you hear? German officer . . ."

"I've heard about it. Stop yelling."

"How? The paper's just arrived."

"I don't know," she said gravely. "Somebody threw it through the window."

"So you've seen it. And did you see the picture?"

"At least now everyone can recognize you," she said.

"You think so? They seemed a little blurry to me. If you agree, I could sue them. I could ask for new pictures. I don't know how you call that. Do you think I should sue them?"

"I don't think anything."

"They must've been sozzled when they took the pictures. Those animals! But I could initiate a change. I know the man from the paper. I worked for his uncle. A hell of a man. A builder. He fell into a lime pit. Rest in peace. What do you think?"

The silence continued. Only then did I notice her being dark with anger and blue in the face like a heart patient. Out of excitement, I thought.

"I know how you feel," I said and stroked her hair. "Take some valerian, and let's read the paper."

I still have it. Besides the diploma, it is my only property. I copied everything regarding me and Colonel von Rüchter. I also want to add that I cut out all the pictures and draped them around the house. Here it goes:

"Unselfishly risking himself becoming a victim of furious waves . . ."

"What damned waves?" said the wife through her nose. "And furious on top of it all."

"There were some. You can't say there were none."

"I can because there were none."

"You can't say that the water was still; you can't claim that."

"Of course it wasn't. Rivers flow and can't be still. But there were no furious waves."

"All right," I said. "The river was turbulent. Can I continue to read now?"

"Read," she said. She sat bent forward with her big wiry hands between her knees. Gloomy in the face as if all her ships had sunk. And this is the kind of wife I have, I thought to myself, but I didn't know what she knew. If I had, I would have folded my hands between my knees, too, and wouldn't have stood in front of her straight up like a monument.

"Unselfishly risking himself becoming a victim of . . . waves, Andrija A. Gavrilović, a former South Beach lifeguard in the town of G., in the late evening hours rescued out of the river a regional commander, Standartenführer SS Mr. Erich von Rüchter, who was, prior to the rescue, a target of a treacherous terrorist assassination attempt . . ."

"I didn't hear any shooting on the river," said the wife.

"Neither did I, but the bastards could've attacked him with a knife."

"As soon as he heard a cry for help, waiting not a moment to put his own life in peril in order to save a German officer . . ."

"You didn't know he was an officer. You jumped in after a wholesale merchant."

"I don't know what I thought," I said with anger. I started to resent Julienne's indifference. "That's not important. These are educated people, and they know better than either you or me how to write for the papers."

So I continued to read: ". . . and eagerly responding to his human instincts, Andrija Gavrilović threw himself into the river's choppy waves, and after a long and desperate fight with watery elements, in which, with a high level of efficiency, he showed his professional ability and his bravery, he managed to pull the regional commander Mr. von Rüchter out of the water . . ."

"If those from the forest were any more skillful, I would've saved a dead man."

"If you only had!" cried out the wife. "If you only had saved a dead man!"

"Why, for God's sake? What's with you all morning?"

"Go to the back door and see for yourself."

"What's to see outside?"

"Go and look."

And I did according to her wish. However, it would have been better if I hadn't. It would've been better if I'd never crossed that threshold, if I'd instead dropped dead on the spot. They'd have covered my face with newspapers, instead of having it exposed like that for the rest of the world to see.

I saw, gentlemen comrades, my dog. The same one I had rescued out of the water when it was only a puppy. My only case besides the Colonel von Rüchter. He was swinging from a beam, hanged with a string around his neck. Somebody had stuck the following sign on him:

COLLABORATOR.

I swear it was the first time I heard that word. At first I thought it was some kind of infectious canine disease. Rabies or something similar. People probably killed the dog to stop the disease from spreading. I realized quickly that the dog had neither been refusing water nor frothing, nor had it curled its tail. Therefore, I concluded that it couldn't have been rabies. Even if it had been, they would have shot it and not strangled it. They would have notified me, too. That was our custom. Then I thought that some hooligan kids killed it out of wantonness. That didn't fly either. The kids normally don't hurt dogs. Once in a while they'll molest cats, but dogs never.

I pulled him down and buried him behind the hangar, all the while thinking what might have happened, until I concluded that this act must have been committed by one of those naked maniacs I had chased off the beach. One of them had killed my dog out of revenge. There were such animals. I removed the sign. I was counting on asking someone about its meaning, which would have also uncovered the nature of the incident. I could not ask just anybody, however. I had a presentiment that it didn't mean anything good. It was just a matter of form. It sounded offensive, like a curse. But I could never imagine that it meant "a turncoat, a degenerate, and a pile of shit," as I later on found out from others, as well as from Comrade Ozren every time he was angry. When he was in a better mood, the word meant "an accomplice to the enemy."

I decided to ask Andraš. He, however, did not stop by that day nor the following week. I was already dressed in my uniform and ready to appear as a lifeguard again. Everything materialized as I had dreamed of, but then again I was not content. It was true that the shore was the same one, the faces were the same, and even the river was the old one, torpid and lazy as ever, as if the drowning of one German officer had depleted all its strength. Then again, nothing was the same anymore.

At first, the children stopped coming. One would have thought that now they would start rushing in hordes since my ratings were high. But there were no kids at all. Empty. Only two weeks later did I meet Kole, the one who pretended to be drowning in front of the inspectors. He tried to avoid me. I ran in front of him.

"How are you, Kole? I don't see you at the beach anymore."

He looked at the ground, avoiding my gaze. He said his father forbid him to go.

"And why is that?"

"He's afraid I would drown."

Something like shivers ran down my spine. "You drown while I'm still alive and watching over this river? What is your father thinking?"

"I don't know. He just won't let me."

"It seems to me you're lying, Kole. Are you?"

"I'm not, Uncle Andrija, I swear."

"You are, Kole. You are."

He didn't answer. He just turned around and ran.

On the same day I met another boy. I've forgotten his name now. I asked him where he'd been lately.

"Nowhere," he said, staring at his shoes.

"Is your father afraid as well?"

"My father's not afraid of anything. He's not a coward like some."

"Then why's he not letting you come to the beach?"

"Just because."

"You see. He's scared."

"He's not!" the boy yelled and stepped back. "He says you're the enemy's servant and a traitor to the Serbian people and that honest people and patriots can never be friendly with such shit."

"What traitor?" I shouted. I could not collect myself. "What kind of a damn traitor am I? Whom did I betray?"

"You pulled that German colonel out of the water. That's what kind!" He spat and ran away.

So that was it. Neither the river nor the beach had changed, but the people had. The world alienated itself from me, turned its back, pretended it did not see me, barely even answered my greetings, and talked to me only officially and out of necessity. Lots of things became crystal clear. Among them, that word: COLLABORATOR.

I came back to the boathouse, ill. I cried and sobbed along the way, hiding my face against the walls. But I almost forgot the following incident. On my way back home, I ran into Ostoja, a former cop who at that time worked as a financial inspector. He was dressed in his uniform. I raised my hat to greet him—I was wearing my uniform, too—but he turned his head, spat, and started to walk quickly away from me. "Honest to God, you're not gonna spit at me, too," I said to myself. I caught up with him and grabbed him by the shoulder.

"What do you want?" he asked.

"What do you think, Ostoja? Do you think I would come to your home and spit on your dining table?"

"I don't know what you're talking about."

"I'm talking about your spitting on the beach."

"I spat on the ground, not on a table."

"People eat on this beach just like you eat at your table."

"So what?"

"You understand that I could write you up?"

"So that you could submit it to your colonel?"

I was in shock. "What colonel?"

"The one that you rescued out of the water and now are going around shaking his hand."

"Are you crazy? I haven't seen the man since then."

"That's what you say."

"So I'm a collaborator?"

"You know it best."

I lost my head and grabbed him by his collar. "And what are you?"

"The financial inspector. What else?"

"An inspector who works for the Krauts. And you're not a collaborator, but I, who work for the people without asking who and what they are, now I am one. Now I am a collaborator, traitor and mere rubbish."

"I don't work for the Krauts but for the county and only because I have to survive somehow. And you work for the German army because you like it. You rescue them out of the river so they can kill us."

My head became cloudy. He took the opportunity to push me aside and leave. He was in a uniform like me, but he stood somehow clean and proud. I found Julienne sitting at home. She looked as if she had a fever, too. I asked what the matter was.

"Why do you ask? You know what the matter is."

"No, I don't," I said. "I don't know anything anymore."

"Then go and ask your son."

My heart trembled. I took the boy in my arms and asked him. I noticed his black eye. He'd been in a fight. That wasn't so terrible. Why such a rumpus then? Even the grown-ups were fighting all over the place. The children could do no better when they had us as an example. People used to fight even during peacetime, and that was nothing compared to this mess. Who could sit in peace when everything around you was shooting and exploding? I was barely able to make him tell me what the matter was, so that at least I could appease Julienne, when the boy burst into tears.

He said they'd been playing war games. They got together, as usual, and started to divide into armies. One said he wanted to be a partisan, and then another yelled he was going to be a partisan, too. Someone else wanted to be a Russian, another one either an American or English, just like the Anglo-American army. The French and Italians didn't count for anything. When Andrija asked them what he was going to be, they said: "You're a Kraut and a traitor." "I don't want to be a Kraut and a traitor," refused Andrija. "I'm always a Kraut and a traitor." "You have to," they said, "otherwise we won't have anyone to fight against." Andrija was inflexible. He was either to be a Russian or an American or nothing at all. "You can't do that," they said. "We have to have traitors because without them we can't play the game." "Why do we need traitors," asked Andrija, "when we have Germans? I could possibly accept being a German, but never a traitor." "Then you can't play!" Of course, little Andrija yearned to play. "What if for once," he asked, "I was allowed to be something else besides the traitor, so that we could all fight?" "Then there would be no one to beat on when we win," said the rest of the kids. "But why always me?" lamented my Andrija. "Why always me?" "Because," they said, "your father is a degenerate and a traitor!" "Whose father is a degenerate and a traitor?" "Yours!" "Whose?" "Yours!" And that was the end of the game. Then came the fight and the black eye. There were a bunch of them and my Andrija was by himself. But even when he agreed to play, it was not much better. It was somewhat manageable while they were warring, although they were running after my Andrija, who was playing a traitor, more than after those who were playing Germans. At the end they would raise a great racket, yell out "long live the liberation," "down with Fascists," or "death to the traitors," and then they would only tie down the "Krauts," since as soldiers they were protected by the convention, and as for my Andrija, who was not protected by anything, they would beat the living God out of him.

"Why didn't you tell me?" I reprimanded my wife.

"How could I tell you when you wouldn't allow us to say anything against your colonel?"

"What does my colonel have to do with this? And since when is he mine? I didn't give birth to him, did I?"

"You saved his life. It's the same."

"I saved a human life, not a colonel!"

"And what kind of human? A Kraut."

"There were no Serbs or Krauts for me. All I care about is who's drowning and who isn't."

"Well, if you continue like that, you're gonna be the one who is drowning," she said. "You'll see when our people come."

"What are they? Who are 'our people'?"

"Partisans."

"And where am I, God damn it? What about me? Where do I belong?"

"You're theirs. A collaborator."

Later on, she felt sorry for what she'd said. "I don't think personally," she uttered, "that you're a collaborator, but I'm just telling you what the others think. If something doesn't change soon, it's gonna ruin us all." Then silence. She became quiet and looked at me as if I were already sitting in court as a defendant. I ran out of the house. Am I crazy? I thought. I didn't know what to do. In my head a pneumatic drill was at work. Just like the one my old boss Constantine Negovan had at his building site. This one in my head sounded exactly the same: col-lab-o-ra-tor, col-lab-o-ra-tor, col-lab-o-ra-tor! I could already see myself hanging with a noose around my neck and my tongue sticking out as in a jest. I pictured someone throwing stones at my little Andrija, my wife's hair bobbed short, so short her scalp actually glistened. Suddenly I fell into such an anxious state that I decided I would end my life right there on the spot. I thought of jumping into the river. I thought I would tie my legs and hang a rock around my neck, to counter my lifeguard expertise. Then I would head straight into the water. I thought at least they would leave my boy in peace. As far as my wife, if they really wanted, they could shear off her hair. Hair grows back fast, but a head does not.

If anyone was guilty, it was only me. But then again, why? What was I guilty of? That I rescued a man? The man was German, the enemy, a conqueror. What of it? Once in the water, he ceased to be all that, and became merely a man. The water cleansed him, christened him. He became a drowning man, and instead of an invader he was a victim; the water engulfed him completely. He was not a German anymore either. He was a nobody. A drowning man. A mere floating straw in the water. Then I thought, slow down, Andrija. Maybe, deep down there in the water, he did indeed become a human being again, but you, on the other hand, changed from a human being into a nonbeing, into a degenerate, a traitor to your nation. You'll hang on a tree. You will, because once the colonel reached dry land, he changed back into a German, into an enemy and a conqueror. The water neither cleansed him nor christened him. It only made him worse. Straight for the noose then! Straight for the gallows! Only me? Who else? You are the traitor.

I wish to pause for a moment and transcribe what Socrates the Greek has to say about this topic. It is not altogether about me, but, indirectly, it touches upon my situation as well. Here it is:

> Socrates: Come hither, Meletos, and let me ask a question of you. You think a great deal about the improvement of youth?
>
> Meletos: Yes, I certainly do.
>
> Socrates: Then tell these gentlemen here, who is it makes them better? It is clear that you know, since you care about it. You have found the one who corrupts them, as you say, and you bring me before this court here and accuse me; now then, say who makes them better, inform the court who he is! Do you not see, Meletos, that you are silent, you cannot say? Yet does it not seem disgraceful to you, and a sufficient proof of what I am saying, that you care nothing about it? Come, say my good man, who makes them better?
>
> Meletos: The laws.
>
> Socrates: That is not what I ask, my dear friend; but what man, who in the first place knows this very thing, the laws?
>
> Meletos: These people here, Socrates, this jury.
>
> Socrates: You mean, the gentlemen of the jury here are able to educate the young and make them better?
>
> Meletos: Yes indeed.
>
> Socrates: All of them, or only some?
>
> Meletos: All.
>
> Socrates: By Hera, you speak excellently and mention quite an abundance of benefactors. Well, what then? What of the people here listening to us, do they make the young better or not?
>
> Meletos: Yes, they do, too.
>
> Socrates: What about the Councillors?
>
> Meletos: The Councillors, too.
>
> Socrates: Indeed, Meletos, is it possible that the Commons corrupts the younger generation? Or do they also make them better, all of them?
>
> Meletos: They do.
>
> Socrates: Then the whole nation of the Athenians, it seems, makes them beautiful and good, except me, and I alone corrupt them? Is that what you say?
>
> Meletos: Yes, this is what I say.

Socrates: (Says something unimportant, and then continues.) That would be some great fortune for the young ones if only one man corrupts them and everyone else does not.

So I ask you, too, just the way I was asking and tormenting myself back then on the beach, what about others? Did they hang the doctors who cured those same Germans, our doctor, for example, who treated Colonel von Rüchter? No, of course not, because he was obligated by his medical profession. Did they thrash bakers who provided the Germans with bread, merchants who sold them merchandise, waiters who served them food and drink in the restaurants, and railroad engineers who moved their trains? Did all of them have a board around their necks with the word "collaborator" painted on it? I can attest they did not. Many a board would have had to be made. But it was easier this way, to place it around my neck only. Everyone else was an honest patriot, everyone but Andrija who was a villain and a traitor. But this, Andrija, is not the same, one might say. Everyone else was only doing his job. Even under occupation, one must continue to live and feed the children; the children would later on become the masses, Comrade Ozren's proletariat, as he liked to call it. If one grain falls into the hands of the enemy, it does not mean that the whole harvest will be spoiled. And me? What was I doing? I did nothing else but perform my job. My job was to save people from drowning, and save them I did. I admit that considering the shape I was in, unemployed and with no future prospects, I would have rescued even a most fiendish devil if he'd been crying for help. I would have pulled him out with my teeth if I had to, gentlemen comrades. I have even read in the newspapers about Germans rescuing Brits out of the water and vice versa. It was considered an act of good faith to throw someone into the water and then to rescue him and send him to hard labor. But my case was called an act of collaboration.

I didn't jump. At that time I still did not entirely comprehend my offense nor realize its gravity. I thought I had nothing to be ashamed of and nothing to worry about. Furthermore, it would have been a little awkward, considering my calling and my reputation, if I'd drowned myself. If a conductor or a restaurateur were in question, for example, it wouldn't have been half as bad. But for a lifeguard, it didn't sound good. I left the river to look around for Andraš and told him everything.

"Better you saved a rock than a German colonel," he said and passed me the newspapers. "Look."

I looked, but saw nothing. German troops occupied Brza Palanka, exchange of telegraphs: Reich Leader to Il Duce, Il Duce to the Reich Leader, Reich Leader to Teno, Teno to the Reich Leader, Teno to Il Duce, Il Duce to Teno, just as if they were telegraph operators and not presidents and prime ministers. Then, Banja Luka occupied again, an order to begin a manhunt in Bulgaria (here we finally had become cannibals), fierce fighting in Italy, Moscow's face slapping of the Polish government in exile, invasion into hell (I knew we would make it there but didn't know exactly when), Reich Leader hosts General Andrey Vlasov, winter help—every kind of blabber possible.

"There's nothing about me," I said and returned the paper to Andraš.

"No, but there's something concerning you."

At the spot where he was pointing his finger, it said:

"Accomplices of bandits who viciously attacked Standartenführer SS Erich von Rüchter, *Kreiskommandant* in the town of G. arrested." And stated underneath was the following: "During the investigation conducted in the last few days, German army authorities arrested ten individuals, proven to have actively helped Communist bandits in their recent assassination attempt on the commander-in-chief of the region of G."

"And you saved this Erich."

"It wasn't written on his forehead that he was an enemy."

"And if it have been, if you knew?"

"How could I have known?"

"I ask you, if you knew, what you do?"

(I would have rescued him; I would have rescued a devil himself if he were drowning. First and foremost, I was a lifeguard.)

"I suppose I wouldn't. I could explain everything," I said.

"No explaining for me, I know what happened, but how explain to others? You not go around and explain everything to people personally. Even then, not everyone believe."

"That's true."

Before I left, I asked Andraš if he was going to stop by my home again. He answered he was too busy, so he could not.

"So you, too, Andraš?"

He writhed and blushed with apparent uneasiness.

"See, Andrija, my family. My kids go to Serbian schools. You understand? Say you understand?"

"I understand; how could I not? What did I do to God for him to annihilate me to my roots? That's the only thing I don't understand."

Since those newspapers arrived in town, and it was already September of 1944, there was no tranquility for me anymore. The beach was loaded with Krauts. There were no civilians except for those degenerates from the county. All honest folk were at Zemba's beach. And he was trying to protect me. He kept saying, "He's not theirs, people. I know him, he's ours." It didn't help. I was a traitor, and that was that. A day or two later, the order arrived for my beach to be closed to our people—even though none of our people were coming anymore—and I was to watch out only for German soldiers. There was no way they would have time to enjoy swimming, I thought. It was just a matter of time before the Russians would storm across the Danube, and rumor had it that the partisans were already liberating nearby villages with banners and brass bands. I was pleased. I thought the Germans would fire me soon, and then everyone would see that I had nothing to do with the enemy. To add to my misfortune, the damned colonel had ordered to keep me employed. Out of gratitude, supposedly. Screw such gratitude if as a result my head wasn't safe on my shoulders. But who could say no to them? They even gave me a pay raise. It didn't matter, however. As if you could buy something with dinars in those days. But the worst thing was that instead of my county uniform, they had me wear a German uniform used for the civil servants.

That same night, some ruffians broke every single window in the house. If we hadn't slithered under the bed, we wouldn't have survived. I awoke late the next morning. I had nightmares the whole night. Some people had gathered around me, threw rocks at me and yelled: "Down with the collaborator!" I awoke with a fright and saw my little Andrija already dressed. My wife was hurriedly stuffing clothes into a suitcase.

"Where?" I asked.

"Me and Andrija to my mother's, and you as you wish."

"Wait!" I jumped. "I'm going, too!"

"Where are you going?"

"To Kreiskommandatur. To thank them and resign my post."

She kissed me. I could see she cared for me. She said her nerves had given out and asked me if I was serious.

"Of course I'm serious."

"Why don't we leave right this second then? Why do you have to report to them?"

I explained to her that in the case where I left without reporting, the way they were so tidy, they might consider me a deserter and then have a warrant on my head. We had enough difficulty with our people; we didn't need even Germans on our back.

She realized the danger of our situation.

"Go," she said. "And for once in your life, try to be smart."

I dressed in my civilian clothes, wrapped their uniform in newspaper, gathered all my papers and the keys of the house, tickets, some remaining money, and rushed over to Kreiskommandatur. Some *Volksdeutscher* received me. He knew Serbian and was really amicable.

"You," he said, "Gavrilović, are the one who rescued Mr. Colonel."

"Yes, I am," I said. Damned be the day when I saved him.

"And you are employed with us as *Strandwächter*?"

"As what?"

"As a beach watcher."

"Yes, and also as a lifeguard. But I can't do it anymore. I just came to thank you."

"That's a pity," he said. "Just when we have a medal for you."

"What medal?" I asked with alarm. "What medal?"

"More like a badge actually. *Lebensrettungmedaille*. It's given out only on special occasions and for great deeds, such as saving lives. Herr Standartenführer went through a lot of trouble to obtain one for you because after all you're not a German citizen. In spite of that, the badge has arrived just today."

"You said the medal!"

"Badge, medal, what's the difference?"

"By God, there is a world of difference to me. This is a state decoration and not a mere pin made of brass!"

"Well, in any case," he said, "it makes no difference to you. It's given only to our active employees."

"That would be me," I said.

"Unfortunately, you're not. You've just resigned."

All my troubles in vain. I asked to at least see it. "Why not?" he said. He opened his drawer and took out a small box. He opened it and, lo and behold, there was the medal. The engraving was a circle with a German two-headed black eagle inside. On it, it was written: ERINNERUNGSMEDAILLE FÜR RETTUNG AUS GEFAHR.

There, and only at that moment, could one say that I became a collaborator. Never before, only at that moment. I don't know if anyone would understand. Possibly some forester who was secluded for years among mountains and never received a decoration, possibly only he would understand me. I have never before in my entire life received or seen one, neither a written acknowledgment nor a pin, and neither had I expected to get one even if I had rescued half a town. How could I resign then?

"All right," I said. "Regarding that resignation. I really don't know for sure. I wasn't completely certain. I just came to see how everything stands, to see if you have any replacement, you know? After all, we're all human . . . I came more for general consultation, just in case I had to resign."

"Then you're not resigning?"

"God, no!"

"So why are you bothering me then?"

"I told you. Just for general consultation."

"Then leave me alone, for God's sake. *Los! Los!*"

"All right, all right. I'm going," I said, trying to mollify him. I waited for the medal.

"Leave then, *um Gottes willen!*"

"And what about the medal?"

"There's no problem as long as you're employed. However, we don't just give out the medals the way you imagine it. With us, it is a public ceremony. We'll inform you of the date. *Auf Wiedersehen.*"

"*Auf Wiedersehen.*"

So I didn't resign. I didn't mention the medal to my wife, no way. I lied to her that I arranged everything, but that we had to wait a day or two until they could find a replacement for me. "Only a day or two, and not a minute longer," she said. I agreed. I didn't want to lose my life because of the medal.

The cannons were still quiet, and the Germans did not seem overly disconcerted, as is often the case right before retreats. I remember

1918. Everyone seemed hard-pressed with something, like an asthmatic. Everyone talked quietly in a whisper. Everything was dying away, waiting, listening. I was dying away as well, waiting, listening.

With my luck, I was afraid the Germans would leave before I received my medal because who was going to find them again. I hoped that as soon as I got my medal I would pack Julienne and my little Andrija into a horse and cart, and flee straight to my in-laws until things settled down and the plague let up. It wouldn't chase after me. There were plenty of others, plenty of those degenerates from the county office. They had blood up to their elbows. And what had I done? I had barely soiled a pinky, and then others had pushed me into the mud. I was a small collaborator compared to them.

"What are you waiting for?" asked my wife. "What did you prick up your ears for?"

"I'm listening for our cannons," I lied. I was waiting for an automobile to arrive from the Kreiskommandatur. A day passed. The next day was Sunday. We were in the month of October. Nothing from the Kreiskommandatur. The wife was getting impatient, almost starting to bite. Kept asking, "When are we leaving?" "A little bit longer," I said. "Seems quiet enough." "That's what I'm afraid of," she said. "Nobody's saying anything; they're just looking at me strangely." "How strangely?" "Like the way you look at a young chicken on Sunday morning." "They have nothing to do with you. I'm the collaborator. But don't you worry. Everything will clear up." "Nothing will clear up," she said and started to cry. "There'll be no time for explanations." Then she started to tell stories about how people in villages were organizing meetings and holding public hearings for traitors, who, according to her, were shot immediately after the sentence. "That's just propaganda," I said. "It's not propaganda; this is what the refugees said." "What refugees?" "The refugees, those who want to put the traitors on trial." "That's clearly all just propaganda because they're the ones who profit from public unrest."

Somehow I calmed her, but myself I could not. It was already Monday and the second day, and still there was no word from the town. Every once in a while, Julienne would pick up the suitcase, ready to leave. "All right," I said finally. "One more day. If tomorrow nothing happens and they don't find a replacement, I'll go back to the

Kreiskommandatura and inquire again. Then we'll leave straight to your parents." The next morning I left her crying and headed back to the same place where I'd been three days ago.

The disorder was tremendous. You couldn't pass through, for so many crates and merchandise. In the yard, archives were in flames. Soldiers were running back and forth, throwing bundles of paper into the fire. Black smoke had risen and spread all the way to the gates, stinging my eyes. The gates were wide open, so you could see everything inside like in a theater. The guard was curt with me and wouldn't let me in. It was worthless me telling him that I was there on business—*dienstlich!*

"Dienstlich gibt es nicht mehr!" he said, trying to push me off with his Shmayser machine gun. *"Es ist aus, Schluss siehst du es denn nicht selber? Machen wir, dass wir fortkommen!"* meaning they were done with business and leaving.

To get the medal, I had memorized what to say:

"Ich komme wagen dem Medaillen, Herr Feldwebel, Erinnerungme-daillen!"

"Medaillen? Medaillen?" he cried out. *"Was für eine Medaillen? Hau ab, sag ich dir, sonst verpasse ich dir eine Medaillen, das du dein Zeben lang in der Frese trägs!"* Loosely translated, he said I was to go to hell, and that he would give me my medal upside my head.

I moved away. I realized he was uptight, and the machine gun could go off by itself. I retreated to the passageway across the street where I had a clear view of the entrance to the Kreiskommandatura. I counted on seeing the *feldwebel* with whom I'd arranged everything about the medal and even possibly the colonel himself. I would've told them that I didn't need a ceremony, considering their predica- ment and retreat, and that they could just hand me the medal, and then we would be done. I waited a long time, waited and waited, and nobody showed up. Inside was full of rubble, everything was burning in flames. They started to dump papers through the windows into the fire. The wind blew some of them and carried them out of the gate, but nobody seemed to care, as if those were not government documents but psalmbooks and religious calendars. As a government official, sorrow spread over me, but as a patriot I exulted. And, mind you, is this the way a traitor would think?

At last, I spotted a petty officer whom I knew from the beach. He was always considerate and courteous. He was pushing a motorcycle. I approached him just as he started the engine.

"*Entschuldigen Sie! Entschuldigen Sie!*"

"*Was wollen sie?*" meaning, "What do you want?"

"*Eine Medaillen!*" I said.

"*Velche Medaillen?*" "What medal?"

I explained quickly. Herr Standartenführer. Drowning. Water. Moonlight. Bandits. Almost alive. Pictures in the newspapers. An important thing for both nations. Fervent service. *Und So.* Medal.

He cursed, pushed me against the wall, jumped on the motorcycle, and sped away.

I realized everything had become madness, and in such circumstances one would have a hard time to assert his rights. But still, I didn't give up on the medal. I had no other evidence of my capability. I had a newspaper article and the diploma, without a doubt, but a decoration was something else. All right, it was not really a decoration, but a medal nevertheless. That meant honor, acknowledgment. I was taken into consideration and counted on.

At that moment I heard the cannonade for the first time. The Germans stopped, their ears pricked up. And from somewhere, not too far away either, it was roaring as if empty barrels were rolling down a hill.

"*Kanonen!*" said the guard.

Cannons! Russians! Our troops! My heart suddenly leapt and fluttered out of my chest. In an instant I had completely forgotten about the medal. Who cared about pins and medals when freedom was approaching? I would receive another badge, but this time from our people. The Germans would never drown again in our pretty rivers, but our national masses might. What else could a lifeguard ever want?

This was what I was thinking when I heard the cannons. Was this how a traitor and a collaborator would reason? At the first sound of the artillery barrage, these people were only thinking how to get away from you, our valiant liberators.

The situation was such that I abandoned the idea of receiving the medal. Julienne had most likely gone out of her mind when she heard the roaring, and I thought I would not be able to delay her any longer. And for what? I'd already said good-bye to the medal. I still had the newspaper and that was something, too. It was more sensible to think about the head on my shoulders. People used to say that the period right after liberation was the most challenging one, and that during that time one had to be really smart. Later on people would cool off and a man would somehow get through.

I hurried home. Everywhere the stores were locked up, windows barred, and blinds drawn. In General Putnik Street, however, there was a great commotion. I didn't know what all those people were doing in front of the Manojlović and Son store. I wondered who could be so anxious to buy and sell at such a time. Only when I got a little closer did I see people bringing the merchandise out and yelling: "Down with the vassals! Hang the bloodsuckers! Down with the black marketeers and speculators! Death to the German hirelings!"

I immediately realized what the matter was, so I left unnoticed, and, walking through alleys and passageways, I arrived home safely. There, instead of my family, was a letter.

"Andrija, I didn't dare to wait any longer. They were looking for you here, saying they were corralling the traitors. Zemba was able to get me out. You do what you please, but don't follow us because if you do, you might implicate us. Zemba sends his regards and recommends you to not follow us as well. He was great help, and you have to be grateful to him for the rest of your life. He advised me to ask for a divorce until this chaos is over, and later we can easily get married again. This is the best solution for our little Andrija. You see in what kind of crap you have thrown us. We have to go now. Down with the degenerates and the traitors. Death to Fascism, freedom to the people. Your former wife Julienne greets you and loves you."

Well, I thought, she loves me and that's most important. That thing about degenerates and traitors, she probably had to write down, just in case a foreign eye would see it. But what would happen to me? Where could I go? I must go somewhere. I couldn't stay. They could come back and check again. Now, in any case, no one is working; they're just looking for some scapegoat, someone who would pay for the last four years of paucity and terror. I would be an easy target. The big guys have already fled for sure. The mayor wasn't gonna wait for them at his office. Gendarmes at least have guns. The Germans were protected by the Hague, and if the convention failed, they still had guns. I didn't, and if I did, I wouldn't know what to do with them.

I'm a lifeguard. That is my profession, not killing, but saving lives. I was doomed and that was all.

But, miraculously, I was not scared anymore. Something had snapped inside of me, and I didn't care. I would not even have fled had it not been for little Andrija. I didn't want him to know that his father was snuffed out as a traitor. He would've been scared all his life. No way, I thought, that I won't allow. I started to pack, but I didn't have much. I filled a bag with some food, newspapers, ten of them—all with my picture in them—and my diploma. I threw away the frame because it was easy to break. I planned to buy a new one if I survived. Then I left. I didn't even look at the beach and the river. I'd had enough of them both.

I went straight across the bank onto the main road. There was already a column of people there, dragging themselves along—fleeing. Wagons loaded with bales, full of belongings, and with people sitting on top. Some of them were hugging cuckoo clocks and some hangers. Children were in washbowls and laundry hampers. Every so often, a truck with an awning would pass, probably belonging to the army, but German motorcycles were everywhere. The infantry walked along the ditches on both sides of the road, one by one, covered with dust and mud. A lot of them wore bandages on their heads and used tree branches as crutches. They still had their Shmayser machine guns; they didn't let go of them. All those people were pushing west. "The Russians are coming! The Russians are coming!" yelled out a woman until they shoved her into the muck. Well, then, I thought, they surely did deserve it.

A cannonade was heard, and behind along the hilltops, pretty far away, the machine guns rattled. *Rat-tat-tat, rat-tat-tat, rat-tat-tat.*

I walked beside a truck for a while. It crawled along the jammed road. I yelled out at them if I could jump up somehow. "No way," howled some financial inspector, "don't you see we're sitting on each other's heads!" "Please, there is probably room for one more." "No. Get away. Get lost."

The truck sped up. I clung to its body.

"Let me up!" I screamed. "I'm yours."

"Ours?"

"Yours! An occupier."

"Go to hell!" shrieked the inspector and stepped with his heels on my hands, almost breaking my fingers. I fell into the mud, but I got up right away. My hand was hanging oddly, but it would recover again, I thought—it did recover later on in Germany, but not fully. I could not give up; I had to go on for my little Andrija. The truck was the last one that carried civilians. You could still count on reaching the West in it, but those in the wagons would barely make it to the next village. But this was their goal anyway. For them it was not necessary to flee the country; they only wanted to leave the city. They were fleeing from the front, and not from the national liberation.

I darted for the truck again and hung on to the fender. Just when the inspector was ready to step on my other hand, the truck cut short, the inspector swayed, went over the railing, and dropped into a puddle. He deserved it; he deserved to go to perdition! I pulled myself up and held on to the railing, and since I had my chest pressed against it and that fiend the inspector was still rolling in the mud, I tried to fling my leg over and land on the truck bed, when those inside suddenly swarmed at me. And now you see what kind of people you have and for whom you have fought for four years, and for four years had to roam through the woods, starve and eat roots and leaves. You may not believe me, but I swear on everything dear to me since I have nothing else, but those inside swarmed at me like at the worst vermin. They were pushing me with their legs and arms, calling me a beast, a collaborator, and a national traitor. And that fiend inspector had jumped onto my back and would not let go.

"What are you trying to do, you beast of a man?" he screamed into my ear.

"Be a Serb now, be a patriot now!"

Luckily, some German petty officer appeared on the scene to try to end this chaos that was thwarting the German retreat. I kept yelling: "*Hilfe! Hilfe!*"

He asked: "What does he want?" nodding at me. "*Was ist los? Was will denn der?*"

"We don't know, Mr. Sergeant," said the degenerates and traitors. "*Wissen wir nicht, Herr Feldwebel! Wir haben ihn noch nie gesehen,*" meaning that the bastards had never seen me before. I knew at least two of them: Pera the Cudgel, who was a gendarme, and one called Kurajica, a refugee from Lika who did something for the town hall. I used to let the latter one use the cabins for free, and now he pretended not to know me. Bloody Devil's servant!

"Ich gehöre zu ihnen!" I was yelling in German out of despair. "I'm yours, I'm yours!"

"Zu wem?" asked Feldwebel. "Whose?"

"Yours."

"Ich verstehe uberhaupt nichts!" he said not understanding me.

"Yours," I said in Serbian. I started to mix Serbian and German, not knowing what I was talking about anymore or what I was doing or thinking. *"Ich bin ein kolaborateur der deutschen!* I am a degenerate and a traitor, a *Vërrater!* I am one *Verkaufte* soul! *Ein Dreck,* a national *Dreck!"*

I took out the newspaper, showing to the sergeant the rescue out of the water, desperate fight, bravery, the promised medal, and telling him that it was not right to treat a collaborator and traitor like this as if there were not room amongst them for an honest man. I blabbered all kinds of things but never let go of the truck.

"Steig auf!" ordered at last the Kraut, meaning get in. *"Los, spring auf!"*

I jumped in. The truck headed for the West.

So long and good-bye, Mother Serbia!

■ □ ■ □ ■

CHAPTER SIX

SO THIS IS HOW, GENTLEMEN COMRADES, I ENDED UP IN WEST GER-
many. Since then a lot of water has flowed under the bridge. To best
describe my state of mind since my arrival here, I will use that Greek,
Socrates, who it seems knew everything: "What a life should I lead,
at my age, wandering from city to city, ever changing my place of
exile, and always being driven out!" And if this kind of life was not
suitable to Socrates, then it was even worse for Andrija. It doesn't
matter how much less. I don't want even to mention everything I've
suffered through. Who cares about how one national *Dreck* lives in
exile? I understand that; I'm not stupid. And everything I did here as
an immigrant, a displaced person, and refugee, I've already stated to
Comrade Ozren through numerous declarations. Everything has been
noted either by *protokollarisch* or by my federal inspector Lieutenant
Kulman. I don't want even to mention Dr. Hamm, who needed everything to prepare my defense. "A biographical background of a case
is of utmost importance," he said. "*Lebenslauf.*" Thank God I had
it. The *Lebenslauf* was dreadful, but at least it was mine. It meant I
was somebody. Dr. Hamm said that if my life had been any better, it
would have been dire for my case. "Then what explanation would you
have for the murder? Without a *Lebenslauf*," he said, "where would be
found your 'peculiarities,' your roots? *Die Wurzeln.*"

I led a little better life once I started to work as a lifeguard in
Hamburg. Unfortunately, in the fifth year my hand went bad, the
same one that was crushed on the day our country was liberated from

under the Fascists' boot. While there was money, I visited the doctor's office. Once they declared me disabled and assigned me to watch cabins, there was less and less money and fewer visits to the doctor's office. I wasn't sorry. They didn't do anything to help me. They touched my hand, probed it and pulled it, tugged at it, and finally told me the obligatory *entschuldigen Sie bitte*—it was dead and they couldn't do anything else about it. "Is it ever gonna start working again?" "*Niemals,*" they said, "the tendon is ripped." "Is there a way to exchange it? Nowadays there's an ersatz for everything." "*Entschuldigen Sie,* we can't; we haven't advanced that far yet." They told me they could screw on a hook instead. I told them no, thank you. *Danke.* How would I work then? "You still have your right hand you could use." Basically, their recommendation sounded as if I should pluck my left hand off and toss it into the garbage like a savage. There was no way I would chop my hand off. What would I do then? Even though I couldn't move it in the shoulder and elbow area, at least my fingers were still working. "They won't for too much longer," they said. Then everyone could go to hell, I thought. I wasn't gonna touch it. Let it bark, 'til it dies.

Therefore I couldn't swim anymore. They kept me a little longer to help around the cabins and with the inventory and then let me go. They gave me an *Entlassung* and a month's worth of severance pay. They said, "*Entschuldigen Sie bitte,* good-bye." I moved to another town. I stayed there until they discovered I was a cripple. Then I moved to a third town. I didn't attempt to work as a lifeguard, there was no way—at least I had that much conscience—but I worked at other menial jobs, unless they were too difficult for me to perform. When they would force me to do something harder, I would try to dodge it until they realized I was a partial cripple, and then, of course, *entschuldigen Sie bitte,* and I was out of there.

Finally I found myself in Munich. I reckoned the city was big, people were merry, full of beer drinkers, and it was a place where even Hitler had his roots, so there must be some work for me, too. Until I found something, the way I was living, the severance was going to last me three months. Above all, Munich was closest to home because, gentlemen comrades, some kind of a mood had overtaken me and kept choking me. I was constantly dreaming about the South Beach, but most of all about my Julienne and my little Andrija. I had no news from them. I used to write in the beginning, but never received an answer. The letters must have got lost or they didn't live with my in-laws. During the night I used to talk with Andraš. Zemba was there, too. We were good friends, better than ever before. Even that financial inspector, *Fleischfresser* or the cannibal, the one who sent my hand to the Devil, came to me in dreams once, and even him I did not hate, although I wasn't sure how I would have behaved during the day. In my dream, we talked while the truck headed toward the West. So long and good-bye, Mother Serbia.

Drifting around, looking for a job, I heard from one of my compatriots that Yugoslavia had opened a consulate in Munich and that they'd started a wholesale repatriation. Calling and pardoning every capable hand that hadn't been stained with blood. I hesitated whether to turn myself in or not. I had neither stained my hands with blood nor belonged to any terrorist group, and the years had passed, and I had neither blasphemed against the country nor associated myself with some radical outfit. (Except that I had contributed, out of sheer humanity, ten deutsche marks to Miloje Dragović, who was a corporal in the army of his Highness, our King, in exile, but it is unknown what had happened with that money because the corporal refused to say anything about it when they arrested him for excessive debauchery in taverns.) Therefore, they could attribute nothing new to me, and as far as the old incidents, as our marshal used to say, they had been drowned in water, written off, amnestied—God's bliss in heaven. I thought I could wind up spending the rest of my days by some river, even if I had nothing to do with it professionally. I would have brought back Julienne and Andrija, found some job based on my physical abilities, and what else could a man want in his life?

Because, as I even told Comrade Ozren, things stood as follows: I did cooperate with the Germans, with their colonel to be more precise, and even then, I just rescued him out of water. I am not repudiating this, even though I didn't know whom I was rescuing. He could easily have been a Serb, and then they could have put me on trial for not being there, *nicht war*? I couldn't classify him first, ask for his identification papers, and then jump in and rescue him. So mine was a short collaboration with one German, based on a professional sense of duty. I had nothing to do with anybody else, except through thrashings. That Frost pounded me pretty good. For everything else

I was not guilty, except that I wore their damned uniform for a few days, and even then, excluding the shirt, the uniform was not completely theirs. To be precise, even that shirt was not. It was not a part of the *Wehrmacht* at that point anymore. It was mostly used for civilians and for national traitors. It was more like winter aid. I was only guilty of being too greedy for their shitty medal—for this I could never forgive myself—and for this, if you wish, you can punish me! But anyhow, these were my thoughts as I walked toward the consulate. Never through the streets, but mostly through secluded alleyways and passageways. I was not guilty regarding the pictures either. I neither took them nor requested them. For the words either. Everything was invented so that I, as a Serb, would be humiliated and spat upon. To throw filth at the popular masses and proletariat. I particularly wanted it to be known that I didn't jump into the water in order to save a symbol of the German nation—I don't even know how that was possible when their symbol was a black eagle. But I do know that the jumping ruined me—and as far as some human impulse had pushed me in, that, I have to say is the truth, although I would like to add to it professional instinct as well.

The day was approaching when I definitely had to decide. The money was gone, and I was even without a truck, which they took away for scrap metal. I decided with a heavy heart to turn myself in. They couldn't kill me on the spot. They could shout and yell all kinds of indignities at me—Comrade Ozren took care of that, albeit not from the beginning but later on when we became closer—but I was already used to that. The most important thing was to reach the homeland, and after that what happens happens. It couldn't be any worse.

I had just spotted the tin blazon on the door of the consulate when a chubby red-haired man, all polished and smelling of flowers, grazed by me.

I gaped. Who was that for the love of God? He looked like somebody I knew—I could not discern immediately. I felt I knew his brother. Then it flashed, Herr Standartenführer! Herr Standartenführer Erich von Rüchter! My case! I was speechless, not so much from seeing him, but from not recognizing him. I could not recognize the one and only man I had ever rescued out of the water, the one who was the sole reason I could call myself a lifeguard.

"Herr Standartenführer!" I yelled out. "Herr Standartenführer von Rüchter!"

He froze in place as if shell-shocked. I ran over to him. I didn't know whether to hug him around the neck or, because of all my misfortunes, to strangle that same neck of his.

He turned around. It was him; there was no mistake about it. He looked at me blankly.

"*Was? Ich verstehe nicht?*" meaning to say he did not know me. He asked who I was.

I remembered Zemba and his complaints how the rescued ones had always avoided him. I thought, well, I swear on my mother's grave, you won't do this to me now. Zemba was in a position to denounce them. He had them by the tons. I had only one and even he was trying to weasel out. He hailed a cab, getting ready to run out.

"The South Beach," I stammered out, following after him, and then the taxicab pulled up. I thought he was going to escape me. "River, Gavrilović, unselfishly risking life to rescue a symbol of the German nation." He was already halfway inside the door, my hand on his shoulder. "*Empfang,* we were photographed together Herr . . ."

He waved off the driver, canceling the fare. He was visibly shaken up. He said: "Shut up, fool!"

He led me over to the sidewalk and pressed me against the wall, all the time looking around him. I thought it was a good sign that he called me a fool. It meant he recognized me.

"I'm called Gruber now," he said sternly. "Erich Gruber, and don't call me anything else. Remember: this is not a joke."

"*Gut,*" I said.

"And what's your name now?"

"Me? Gavrilović. What else?" Just because I lost my country, doesn't mean I lost my name.

"*Gut,*" he said, continuing to look around. "Let's go somewhere for a drink and we'll see what to do."

At first I refused, considering that the last time I had a drink with him, I had been as good as dead, but on second thought I changed my mind. It was not his fault that I couldn't handle alcohol. It was also an opportunity to ask him about the medal. It could have been useful for my profession just in case those from the consulate declined my petition.

Now is an opportune time to let you know that I had, out of sheer survival and never out of pride, more than once inquired through various offices about my medal. They always asked me the same questions: "Where are your documents?" "Where is the *Beweis*?" "Do you have any witnesses?" "What witnesses, my good people? It was dark," I would say. "And what about that *standartenführer*? We need him, too." "I don't know." "Then we can't help you. Get out of here." To others I was unable to describe the medal either. "It's not really a medal," I would say. "It was more like a badge, but an honorary one." They had known many different kinds, and even received some of them, for example the Party pin that people used to wear during the May parade, or the pin for the most reproductive mother, so they'd heard of every fucking pin except for mine. The more humane officials treated me as such. Others wouldn't even talk to me. They didn't care what had happened in the past. Neither before nor during the war. "That wasn't *Rechtstaats*. That doesn't count anymore. What happened happened; we don't acknowledge that." "And why not? Who ever heard of a son who wouldn't recognize his father's debts? And your fathers were indebted to me. Not just me, for that matter. They were indebted to the popular masses." "We refuse to acknowledge it." "All right. Never mind that you don't acknowledge it, it's your prerogative, but there are others who do. They acknowledge and remember everything, keeping it all documented and sealed with wax." "That's their problem," they said. "We are working on erasing the past." "I'd like to erase it, too, but I can't," I lamented. "Why not?" they asked. "*They* don't let me." "Well, my friend, then you go and appeal to *them*." And this meant to appeal to *you*.

So I did finally stumble upon a witness. I, of course, didn't want to bring up the subject right away—I was not stupid—but I waited until we found some tavern and he ordered a round of drinks. Then I started:

"So you're not in the army anymore, Herr Standartenführer?"

"Listen to me, Gavrilović," he glared at me. "I am now *Geheimer Rat*. A privy councillor. Geheimer Kommerzienrat Gruber, do you understand?"

"I understand, Herr Standartenführer."

"Geheimer Kommerzienrat Herr Dr. Gruber, you idiot. *Verschtehts du?* And don't you even think about mentioning my real name and rank again."

I understood. He was noted in some black books. Much later, I found out from Comrade Ozren that my benefactor was named in the Nuremberg books. I said good-bye to my medal. This guy wasn't going to appear live in front of any committee.

"*Verschtehts du?*"

"*Jawohl,* Herr Stand . . . Geheimer Rat."

"*Gut.*"

I thought I was not the same person I once was, either. I was not Andrija A. Gavrilović, a lifeguard. I was a refugee, a DP (a displaced person). On top of that, a national traitor, a degenerate, and a quisling. So we were in the same boat. But we were not the same. He was still a gentleman, and I was a nobody. He was already ordering a second round. So he had *Geld,* meaning money, I conjectured. I saw there was going to be trouble. I would get sozzled, and that would be the end of me. My stomach was empty. Every time I met that man, I had to drink on an empty stomach. What a nightmare.

"Also," he asked, "when and how did you end up in Germany?"

"It happened." I didn't feel like confessing.

"There's no bread in communism, huh?"

I got angry. Why not? We Serbs might be communists, but at least we're not the Ottomans. "There is bread, why not, but there's none for me."

"Why not? Did your rivers dry up?" he even joked.

"I'm a national traitor."

"What are you?"

"A quisling, Mr. Privy Councillor."

He started to laugh. He wanted to order another round in that name. He wanted to toast to a quisling. I didn't refuse; I surrendered.

"So Mr. Quisling, why are you a traitor?"

"What do you mean, why?"

"Why did they pronounce you a quisling? Did they put you in the Serbian cabinet before the end of the war?"

Go ahead and mock me, I thought. You're in your own house now.

"Because I rescued *you* out of the water."

"You were a lifeguard, weren't you?"

"I was, mister, but only for Serbs. Not for the Germans. My act counted as collaboration with the enemy."

He laughed loudly again. The way things were going, I realized the fourth round was probably coming pretty soon. My head was already starting to spin. I was embarrassed to ask for a sandwich; I was no beggar, even though I had no passport.

"Collaboration with the enemy on the water," he said choking with laughter. "A naval collaboration, to be more precise. Unbelievable. You Balkans are some horrid people!"

I should have let him drown, I thought. He wouldn't be sitting here calling me horrid. After all, why did they come there if we were so horrid? Why didn't they stay away?

"So you fled, emigrated?"

"Yes, Mr. Privy Councillor."

"And how did you manage here?"

"Not so well."

Then I told him everything. I hid nothing and held back nothing. The drinks drove me on. Hamburg, my dead arm, doctors saying to throw it away, wandering from town to town, low wages, high prices, hoboing, the truck, layoffs, and the last thing left for me: the deep water. Either that or the consulate of the Federal People's Republic of Yugoslavia. I was not sure which was better.

"I'll apply for repatriation, and then they can do with me whatever they please."

"What would they do?"

"Cut my head off. Swish."

"*Dummheit.* And after so many years? For a thing like that? I bet you they don't even know about you. They probably never did. And even if they had heard, after these ten years they've probably forgotten about it."

Then after we downed the fifth round I said, "Maybe this is the case with you people here in Germany, Mr. Privy Councillor. You're a great nation, so it's easy for you to forget. Especially evil. We're small, minute, a handful of woe, so even that has some value for us. Often we have nothing but woe. So we have to savor it and guard it like eyes in our sockets. We forget it only when we die."

"I knew you were out of this world."

Then to confirm my statement, I told him a story, which made him laugh for a long time, the case of Father Grigorije from Novi Slankamen on the Danube. It would not cost you anything to hear this story now as well. It may give you some idea of whom you are dealing with. So I began: "Father Grigorije was called upon to prepare the soul of a certain saddler called Mrkoje for his meeting with God. The good father did come, but in the middle of the prayer, he spilled a whole carafe of wine on the dead man's head. 'This is for you Mrkoje,' he said, 'because you pissed all over me during your baptism. This is for you, to have something to complain about to God, so it wouldn't look like you weren't a Serb.' This is just the way our race is, Mr. Privy Councillor, ill natured."

"If you're afraid," asked the colonel, "why don't you stay here?"

"What would I do here? Die crippled?"

Then he told me not to worry about anything. He would not permit a man who had saved his life to undergo any more suffering. He would recommend me to someone in charge of the swimming pools in Schwabing, which was part of Munich. The man in charge was a lieutenant during the war and a good friend of my benefactor. His name was Venzell, so I eventually reported to him. He also told me that after his house in Ammersee was completed, he would hire me there as a guard. Only under one consideration.

"What consideration?"

"To not say a word about me to anyone."

"To say that I don't know you?"

"You only know Geheimer Kommerzienrat Dr. Gruber."

"*Gut,*" I said. "All right."

I planned on working for a while, or at least until I mended my life and put some meat on my bones. I wanted to come back to my little Andrija and Julienne not as skinny as a pole, but like a man of the world. I couldn't count on looking like what our immigrants to America used to look like, but, nevertheless, I would certainly look more distinguished than I had ever been. I didn't tell him this, however. I just kept thanking him and kissing his hands.

"Thank you, Herr Standartenführer!"

"Drop dead!" he said. "Don't call me that. I have to be grateful to you and not vice versa."

Both of us, I thought, had to thank each other. I pulled you out of the water, and you're going to pull me out of poverty. Any way you look at it, you seem to be like the knot that needs to be untied to get out of the net I was caught in. And that's what happened. This is the reason why I'm sitting here. While he was alive, I couldn't redeem myself in the eyes of my homeland. Not until he returned back to the water, from where I had rescued him, could I plead for me and my past some kind of righteousness and mercy. But then, I ended up in jail, so it made no difference to me.

Upon leaving the tavern, I asked him about the medal.

"*Medaillen? Was für eine Medaille?*"

He didn't remember. These Germans are really a strange sort. They never remember anything. They couldn't remember the war, as if their brains were made out of cannabis. But what engineering! He only remembered after I'd explained to him everything in detail. "All right," he said. "It'll be taken care of somehow. It won't be the same one, of course, since we don't make them anymore, unfortunately, but we'll find something."

"*Gut,*" I said.

My employment in Schwabing, I don't need to go in detail about. It was short and besides I didn't work too hard. That SS Venzell let me do what ever I wanted. He obviously had received instructions. In September, Mr. Gruber, I mean Rüchter, showed up and personally transported me to Ammersee Lake. All I had to do was to take care of the indoor pool and to watch over the house. And be quiet, also. Nobody knew about that little house, not even his wife. He was a family man, and he hoped that I understood that his work required this. I understood. "Once in a while a few people might visit me here," he said. "Mostly friends and their female companions. So. You understand?" "Of course, I do. I know what a brothel is!"

He got angry. According to him I was an ass because this was no brothel, but rather a vacation house.

All right, I thought, but in Serbia before the war we used to call it a brothel. However, I didn't want to argue with him about it.

I don't want to go on about the abnormalities and nuttiness that I saw at this Ammersee Lake villa while I worked there. I already told everything to Comrade Ozren, who could not have enough of it. It all sickened him, he said, but he needed every detail for propaganda.

He wanted to expose the rotten life of the wild bourgeoisie and war criminals while the working class was suffering. As I was telling him, he would get all red with rage, cussing out those "capitalist bastards." If someone from home is interested in this, out of disgust for the revolting way of life of the bourgeoisie and their, as Comrade Ozren used to call them, devilish minions, he can ask Comrade Ozren personally. He knows everything by heart. He even has the addresses of the women who used to come to the villa for relaxation. He said he needed them for documentation.

And so arrived that fatal day on which they say I did the deed. Early in the morning Mr. Councillor had called to let me know he was coming. He called me on the phone. He was going to be alone. He had some important business to attend to. *"Gut,"* I said. He ordered me to get the pool ready. According to him, there was not going to be any racket, so I thought I would at least sleep peacefully on the last night before my resignation. I had decided to leave. I'd put some meat on my bones, and my bank account was full of money. I was coming to you, Mother Serbia.

I cleaned the pool first. Unfortunately I forgot to move the wheelbarrow away, which would later be indisputable evidence. So that the grime would not leak all over, I placed nylon inside the wheelbarrow, but during the trial they would accuse me of doing this intentionally, so if I had had enough time I would have loaded Mr. Councillor inside. The nylon would not drip any blood, and there would be no evidence.

He arrived in his car around dusk. He ordered me to light the fireplace and to meet him at the pool in half an hour. He said he had something for me.

"I have something for you, too," I said.

"All right. I'll see you in a half an hour and we'll talk."

We will, I thought. I planned to thank him nicely and tell him that it was time for me to go home. Auf Wiedersehen.

I had just lit up the fire and was stirring it up with a poker, when I heard him calling me. Suddenly, I realized that everything was similar to the first night when we met. Everything was there: the night, the moonlight, and him calling me for help. The only difference was that on the first night he was not calling my name, Andreas, as he normally did, but was wheezing as if some heavy weight was lying on his chest.

God Almighty, I thought, he's drowning again!

I darted toward the pool with the poker still in my hands; who could think about the poker while a man was drowning. Water was my domain. If he had been in some other mishap, I might not have helped him at all, but since I couldn't put a stain on my profession, I had to save him from drowning.

Mr. Councillor was sinking. The water was illuminated in an indigo light, better known here in Germany as a neon light, which came from the ceiling, so it looked as if he was sinking through the universe instead of the water, and instead of air, he was emitting bloody bubbles. I realized immediately that before changing into a swimsuit, he must have slipped, hit his head on the edge of the pool, and fallen into the water, unconscious. In that case, however, he could not have cried for help. Then who did it? This is not clear to me to this day.

I was already in the water. My crippled arm was a hindrance. Also I was out of shape, heavy, and old age had eaten away my strength. I did manage somehow to pull his head above the water, but I was almost drowning along with him. His head seemed dead, only the blood gushing out of it seemed alive. With my last speck of strength I lugged him over to the edge and propped him up against the steps. Half his body was still in the water and the other half rested on the stone stairs. I felt his pulse. It wasn't beating. Dead. Rest in peace. Then I fainted beside him, almost dead from the effort and fear. When I recovered my senses, Mr. Privy Councillor had slipped away, and was floating with his face and stomach down in the water, arms and legs spread like Jesus.

What happened next, how Mr. Reiner, my benefactor's partner, found me in this state and how I was immediately arrested and accused of premeditated murder, you can ask Comrade Ozren from the consulate of the Federal People's Republic of Yugoslavia. What ruined me was the fact that the poker was smeared with Mr. Councillor's blood and hair, from which Mr. Kulman concluded it was "the blunt object used to inflict a deadly blow." In addition, he, der Geheimer Kommerzienrat Gruber, was not dressed in his swim trunks but in his civilian clothes. I, on the other hand, was wet, so it looked as if he, fighting in agony, pulled me with him into the pool. What was even worse was the wheelbarrow covered in nylon that was found in front of the bathroom and which, supposedly, I would have used to transport the body into the woods. Also, my confession and how I took everything upon myself—even though I was not guilty, as you can see for yourself—how they convicted me, all this exists in the report filed by Comrade Ozren, which he hopefully forwarded as he promised. But I doubt he did. He was angry with me because of the German reparations. (Right before he left me for good, he walked back to the door and said, "So I ask you for the last time, old man, will you *collaborate* with us or not?" "To do what, Comrade Ozren?" "To *collaborate!*" "This, and God be my witness, you shall never live to see. I am not collaborating with anyone anymore. I was a collaborator once, and look what came out of it. I'm done with collaborating. *Schluss!*") But maybe he did send it. Maybe after he heard I was writing this explication, he was not angry anymore. He probably hoped I was going to do as he had directed me. But I won't. I want you to know that I'm not going to follow anybody's instruction. Neither Kulman's nor Hamm's. Especially not Hamm's.

And what my benefactor had for me was the pin. Mr. Kulman had asked me about it, too. He didn't know to whom it belonged. I didn't want to tell him. It was the same one. The same black eagle, the same words: ERINNERUNGSMEDAILLE FÜR RETTUNG AUS GEFAHR. It was shining, all yellow, on the top of the marble bench next to the pool. I didn't take it. It didn't belong to me anymore.

■ □ ■ □ ■

CHAPTER SEVEN

SO THIS IS THE TRUTH AND THE WHOLE TRUTH ABOUT MY CASE, AND during my speech I have not concealed anything, neither great nor small. This is what Socrates the Greek told his judges, and this is what I say to you, my judges. In addition, just as he said, I could say as well: a great prejudice has arisen against me, amongst many of you. Similarly, many a good man has been condemned in the past, and, I am afraid, many more shall be condemned in the future. And if someone should ask, "Are you not ashamed, Andrija, for devoting your life to such a profession, the profession of a lifeguard, which is likely to bring you to your ultimate end?" I would answer such a man as Socrates did: if you think a man who is good for anything ought to calculate his chance of living or dying, and that in his work and his activity he ought not to consider whether he is doing right or wrong, or acting the part of a good man or of a bad, then all his efforts are useless and meaningless. If the capital trial were a few days longer instead of only one, you would become certain of it.

In regard to confessing to a crime which I did not commit, I can honestly say I often wished for it to happen, for that I shall answer upon my death. Since I confessed to the murder, I am as guilty as if I had committed it. And as far as why I confessed it, it must be clear to you from my narrative. There was no other way to cleanse the word traitor from my name. No other way but to pretend to leave Mr. Privy Councillor Gruber where I had rescued him as Standartenführer von Rüchter. Only in this way was I going to be able to take off the sign

COLLABORATOR, the one which had been placed around my neck during the wartime.

I am assuming that the sign is gone now. Everything should be the same as it was. He who should be in the water is in the water, and he who was supposed to be on dry land is on dry land. The dead wait for their destiny in the other world, and the living in this world. I, however, am finished. I am old. I have no future. I don't think I shall live long enough to see freedom again. I have thought about cutting it short, especially after reading the book about that sage Socrates. Not only the book, but the introduction as well. It was stated there that Socrates bathed first, then bid farewell to his sons and his family, and finally ended his life with a cup of poison. His friends tried to dissuade him. "There is time," they told him, "we know of others who drank poison much later, after dusk." For it had been decided at the trial that Socrates must drink a cup full of poison because he was condemned to death. Do you know what Socrates told them? He said that by waiting he would gain nothing but shame because it would show that he was fervently clinging to life, and that there was no reason to prolong it any longer since there was nothing left of it. Then he drank the poison, which had been previously crushed in the cup, lay down, said something more about some rooster that he owed to someone, pulled a blanket over his face and died.

In all honestly, I have to say that I was thinking of doing the same. I even found rat poison in the bathroom. Then I changed my mind. I didn't know its potency. I might survive it somehow and then get crippled even more with some side effects. But there was an even more important reason. It is sinful to take your own life if your conscience is clear. It would be as if God had given you a gift and you took it and spat on it. And I have to say that my conscience is clear. I have cleansed myself from being a collaborator. My Andrija will not be known as the son of a national traitor. Therefore, for this reason, I believe I should be allowed to be buried on the territory of the Federal People's Republic of Yugoslavia, which I plead for in this appeal to all of you, to every member of the committee.

■ □ ■ □ ■

WRITINGS FROM AN UNBOUND EUROPE

For a complete list of titles, see www.nupress.northwestern.edu.

Words Are Something Else
DAVID ALBAHARI

Perverzion
YURI ANDRUKHOVYCH

The Second Book
MUHAREM BAZDULJ

Tworki
MAREK BIEŃCZYK

The Grand Prize and Other Stories
DANIELA CRĂSNARU

Peltse and Pentameron
VOLODYMYR DIBROVA

And Other Stories
GEORGI GOSPODINOV

The Tango Player
CHRISTOPH HEIN

In-House Weddings
BOHUMIL HRABAL

Mocking Desire
DRAGO JANČAR

A Land the Size of Binoculars
IGOR KLEKH